Jackpot Jeans: A Rom-Com Adventure

by

Jeff Whited

Foreword

These affairs took place in the southwestern suburbs of Kansas City in September of 2003, back in an age when people were smart, their phones less so, and six million dollars was a lot of money.

Wednesday the 10th

At Thirsty Mack's Bar & Grill it was "Hump-Day Happy Hour," which meant free Tater Friskies, and so the place was spilling with professional women, many of them spilling from their professional blouses. And by the looks of it, many men were eager to mop up the mess.

Adam Durham was there, along with seven guys from the office. Bachelors all, the others stood tall and grinned like candidates and nodded a lot because nodding suggests confidence and a good temper. But Adam wasn't there to charm the women. He was there because he couldn't dodge *every* social event stemming from his job at Teletech Technologies.

His colleagues clutched their bottles like trophies and chattered about a cool software program and a Spanish supermodel, and it seemed they'd be happy to screw either one. With each gulp their voices got brasher and their adjectives bolder. Adam stayed out of the scrum because he viewed software as a pain in the ass. Supermodels, too, did little for him. As corny as it sounds, he preferred his brand-new girlfriend to them all. There was nothing made-up about Erin Patterson. She looked like the girl in your favorite love song.

He noticed a striking young woman staring at him, unless it was the poster of nachos behind him that tempted her eye. Truth be known, this woman's face was more exotic than pretty, a face to analyze more than savor. The cheeks were so chiseled and the brows so verdant that he wondered if that face might weigh heavy on those who saw it too often, the way a tattoo on a forearm must eventually exhaust its owner. Adam stepped away from the poster and her eyes stayed on him. *Well, this is something*, he told himself. And it *was* a nice moment. He still wasn't used to being handsome at all.

Before they ever spoke, he'd had a crush on Erin Patterson. They went to the same gym, which was old, creaky, and cheap, like most of its members. What had gotten his attention was the way her pony tail bobbled from that little opening in the back of her ball cap as she jogged on the treadmill. During the drudgery of his workdays he thought about that pony tail and those athletic legs and those blushing cheeks, and during the nights he visited the gym hoping she'd be there. Often she was there, and sometimes they smiled at each other. Then one night their arms collided as they grabbed for towels. In a panic, Adam rushed to a recumbent bike. Erin soon took the bike beside his, and they gabbed in a patter fueled by the fear of awkward silences. She was a secretary for a personal-injury lawyer. Adam said he'd once considered a career in law when his dad sued a neighbor because her dog kept stopping by to crap. Erin said she had no dog but was on good terms with Phil, a neighbor's beagle. Adam said he had a great-uncle named Phil who'd once partnered with Lee Harvey Oswald in a three-legged race.

Crossing their view came a tall guy with a self-important posture. Adam and Erin swapped conspiratorial grins, and under his breath he said "Ian Moon" as if the man's name alone was a point of fun.

"He looks so out of place, wearing those flashy suits in a place like this," she whispered while catching a final glimpse.

"He does these financial seminars. He's just here because the meeting rooms are cheap."

"But he dresses like he can afford better."

"He can. His dad's loaded. All those used-car lots. Gerald Moon Motors."

"Ah, that," she said, one brow arched.

"You've seen those dumb commercials, I'm sure."

"Yeah, and so who's the guy that wears the big diaper?" she asked.

"Commander Felix. Always got him crawling around in a playpen, sucking this gigantic pacifier. Don't ask me why. It's just so insane. I mean, I read somewhere he's the guy who does their taxes."

"So, Ian Moon? Hmm." She gazed heavenward. "That family *must* be loaded."

Quietly, Adam said, "He's also here because if you want to rip off old people, you go where they go. He's even doing a seminar on how to win the lottery. Do you believe the nerve of this guy?"

"Good grief," she said.

Finally, a woman who gets me! Finally, he told himself, pedaling vigorously. Oh he loved her so much, the pulse rate on his panel was spiking to deadly levels! Impulsively he asked her out for Saturday night, and with barely much hesitation, she said, "I think I'd like that maybe."

Adam smiled so fiercely that his cheeks ached the whole next day.

Their paths didn't cross until Saturday night when they met outside a Greek restaurant, an obscure gem run by an old couple who dressed in colorful tatters and greeted the customers with their arms outstretched. The place was always deserted and would therefore accommodate easy conversation. He'd long known it would send the right signals to the right woman once he found her. But when that evening arrived, Erin Patterson beheld the building from her seat in her car and broke the news that she'd had Spiro's Gyros for lunch—"What a space cadet I can be sometimes! I mean, I totally forgot about this place for tonight." Instead, she suggested they check out this cool new place she'd heard about called The Remarkable Rib.

Like many Kansas Citians, Adam believed good barbecue could send you soaring straight to the heavens, sauce stains and all. Sadly, on his one visit to The Remarkable Rib, his palate convinced him the ribs had been broiled in England and shipped on a slow boat to America, where they ended up drenched in a barbecue sauce that was bottled alongside Play-Doh at the Hasbro factory. Yet somehow The Remarkable Rib was much in demand. It was first championed by a baseball reporter, and then by a Vegas rapper who was in town to kill a guy, and finally by the boyish pastor of a mega-church nearby. Soon the lines there were remarkable. And that, unfortunately, was the case on his first date with Erin.

At least it was a mild night. Erin looked so angelic in her peach shorts and red top, he didn't mind they were queuing the night away for the reward of dispiriting food. Hell, he'd have eaten at a landfill if she wanted to.

Anxious small-talk filled the opening minutes, much of it a rerun of the news they'd shared at the gym. At the ten-minute mark he sensed the chat was losing steam, a bad sign because several hours remained in the evening, not to mention the rest of their lives together. So he transitioned to a sure thing: his grim childhood. Certainly Erin would find his youthful hardships to be romantic. She'd be glad to learn he'd never been a figure of privilege like that dreadful Ian Moon from the gym. So Adam began at the grimmest point: the tragic death of his mother when he was seven.

It was a loss that floored his father, who'd been wobbly to begin with. Hubert Durham, an unschooled man with tiny talents and a big mouth, had spent twenty years bouncing from one menial job to the next, but the settlement from his wife's car wreck put a merciful halt to all of that. Hubert pledged to live forever off that money, out of respect for the woman who'd propped him up for so many years.

"It was like she'd have died in vain if he squandered the dough," Adam told his lovely date. "Dad was kind of a romantic, if you think about it. He said she wouldn't want him to work because she knew how much he hated getting bossed around by dumb guys. And so when the settlement check came in, he slashed expenses and moved us to this tough area on the Missouri side. I'll drive you there sometime so you can check it out."

"For sure." She lifted to her toes and peered past him. When she saw the front door was still many people away, her lips flattened into a line that was very long itself.

Without the stabilizing presence of his wife and the occasional catharsis of an honest day's work, Hubert Durham lost his mind. Oh, he remained a functioning human being, able to read the funny papers and run errands and fill the ice trays, but soon he looked like a discarded hippie and soon he spent his time on his sad slab of a front porch, waving a fist at the nicer cars that cruised by.

"He believed rich and powerful people got that way by stepping on others and rigging the rules."

"Hmm," she went.

Adam's throat seared from all the talking. He needed a drink by now. Mostly what he needed was for Erin to do some of the talking.

"I mean, the only time he ever felt joy was when a big shot or a senator got arrested. Like, Jim Bakker, the TV preacher with the wife who wore the tinfoil lashes?"

"Tammy Faye?"

He clapped hard. "Good call, Erin! Well, you should've seen my dad light up when that phony got sent up the river. He did this dance in the kitchen, like how Snoopy dances when he's feeling blissful, his nose pointing at the sky. I swear, he'd have thrown a party if he had any friends." Adam paused to work up some lubricating spit. "Yeah, he took a lot of abuse for being so different, and so did I, because he was my dad, you know, and because I was an anxious kid and gangly and four-eyed and all. But the thing is, that worldview was not *that* crazy. That's how the world works. The game *is* rigged. He just let it get to him too much."

She nudged him forward with a forearm, but he had nowhere to go.

To be sure, Erin's reactions so far might seem ominous, but there were circumstances to factor in. For one, that damn line was long, and she was certainly famished by then. Adam knew the food would suck, but he hoped it would restore their blood sugar levels.

"Anyway, he died of a heart attack a couple weeks after I finished high school. The timing was bizarre. An hour earlier I'd finished mowing the lawn, and this girl that went to a Catholic school drove past in a shiny new car. I'd had this crush on her for a long time—yes, Erin, I was a hopeless dreamer, pining after the halfway-rich girl down the block. Anyway, Dad saw me light up as I watched her go by, because he said—I'll never forget it because these were his last words ever to me—he said, 'Boy, just be thankful she's too damn good for you.'"

Erin made an inscrutable sound effect.

Nodding, Adam continued: "Right. It was his way of being a parent for a change, of giving advice, of letting me know he cared. A back-asswards way, but appreciated just the same."

"Yeah?"

"Well, it kind of hurt back then. Heck, I didn't appreciate it for a long, long time. And sometimes still it gnaws at me if I let it. But, anyway, an hour later the poor guy was face down on that porch and I was an orphan."

"Ouch."

"Yeah. Yep. It was, like, relatively weird."

"Was there much of the settlement left?" she asked as they finally made it inside the doors.

"There *was* enough to get me through college without having to take more than a few crappy jobs. You see, my grades were never good enough for scholarships. I was smart but couldn't focus, couldn't sit still, couldn't relax. Then in college this doctor prescribed some pills and life got easier pretty fast. Sometimes I can even sit still now."

"Where do you work?"

"It's just this awful place called Teletech. I think there's something better out there, but I don't know what. And I'm scared to death I'll never know."

"Hmm."

Looking up at the menu board, he gave an understated clap and said, "So, Erin, what's good here?"

Because the dining room was stuffed with tables, those in line had to seep into any spaces they could find, and so the seated diners got subjected to a slow-moving parade of buttocks at nose level. It was a situation that dampened Erin's mood, as had the awful food, because she picked at her expensive half-slab of long ends and the tiresome puddle of beans and never once made a sound effect of pleasure.

Outside, he suggested ice cream. Liquor was an option, of course, but there was something sweet and homespun about hiking to Ben & Jerry's and grabbing a cone. Her shrug was so darling that he couldn't help himself. He swooped in, seized her hand, and whisked her down the sidewalk.

"Durham!"

His smile collapsed.

"Adam Durham! Yo, bro!"

This unwelcome voice sucked his soul straight down from heaven and back into his body at Thirsty Mack's, where his hand clutched not Erin's warm and tender hand but a muggy bottle of beer.

"Say what?" he soon managed.

"Ha, dawg. You spotted her too. The Euro-looking chick over there." The intrusive speaker was Trip, a colleague. He gave Adam a soft slap with the backs of his fingers. "Looks like she's all alone. How's that happen? Unless she's hiding a dinger in those jeans."

"I don't know," Adam said lifelessly; his spirit wished to return to Ben & Jerry's.

"God, even if she was carrying wood down there, I'd be happy to—I mean, no! Not really! Like, scratch that. You never heard that. But no, she's all woman. Look at those knockers. What I wouldn't give. Oh! Hey, so guess what."

"What, man?" Adam often used words like *man* and *dude* and sometimes even *hombre* when talking with guys he wasn't close to; it was his way of saying *I may be aloof, but I'm not a prick*.

"Guess who I saw last night at Starbucks?"

"Who'd you see last night at Starbucks?" he said, playing along for his own amusement. Even though he'd been plucked from a sweet reverie, he realized reality wasn't so bad because soon he'd leave for his second date with Erin, a night that promised to produce its own sweet memories.

"That cute chick you were with the other night when I stopped to chat. Remember? In that parking lot? Erin was her name, I do believe."

"Really? You saw *her* last night?"

Nodding, Trip said, "And this lovely Erin was enjoying frappes or some foamy shit with a tall, freckly guy. An Opie Howard-looking guy. And, I mean, they were *snarfing down* those bad boys. Frothy mustaches were had by all, my friend."

"Wait," stammered Adam, as much as one could stutter on such a tiny word. He got very white in the face or else very red—he knew it was one or the other because he felt clammy yet sunburnt all at once. The questions flooded his throat and tasted salty back there, as if words could weep. He took a dose of his beer. It greased the vocal chords and strengthened his words into a whisper. "You sure it was her?"

Trip placed his slobbery mouth very close to Adam's ear. "It was definitely her, dawg. The same babe you had at Ben & Jerry's on Saturday night."

Adam took a step back and strangled the neck of his beer with both hands. The bottle dangled knee high, like a corpse.

"Man, those foamy mustaches were wild. At one point she kissed his foam clean away. Turned my stomach, to be brutally honest. So, what about you, big guy? You're a free agent, I do believe. You got it in for the foreign chick over there? Except maybe she's waiting for her date. I heard her ordering nachos, and those bastards come on this really big platter, and so probably some boyfriend is running late. But no worries, guy: there's all kinds of lovely snatch in here tonight." With a sweep of an arm, he turned as if to introduce his colleague to the reserves of women. But by the time he turned back, his colleague was gone.

From his car, Adam caught Erin by phone. She was in a hurry, but spaced around a dozen husky sighs she confessed she'd been seeing Ian Moon for a few days now.

"A few days now? You've only been seeing *me* a few days now."

"Sorry I had to be sneaky, but how else—"

"I thought we decided he was a crook. I mean, what am I missing here?" He could hear her shower coming on. The sound of crashing water was crushing to his soul. "Erin, we made those jokes about those rip-off seminars he does. Preying on old people and all."

"He's not a crook. He's very gentle. And those happen to be services they need."

"Right. Like how to pick the winning lottery numbers?"

"There *are* algorithms involved. But anyway, nothing personal, but I like how he's assertive and positive. You're a nice guy, but you're different and stuff. And a bit self-absorbed."

"No way! I say nineteen words a week. Spend a week with me and I'll prove it! You can even count the words!"

"And maybe a little on the dark side. You're working through some stuff, it sounds like. Which is good—"

"Maybe when you grow up like I did and deal with all those mean kids—and mean grown-ups—it can be hard to . . . I don't know."

After a pause, she said, "I think you're drawn to me because I don't have money. And it's a dumb reason to like me is all. It's actually kind of insulting. It limits me."

"I was more into *exalting* you."

"Nobody wants that." She groaned a long one. "Hey, there's nothing wrong with wanting nice things. My apartment sucks. My car shoots out this orange exhaust."

"So the lies, the deceit, it's all for the money?"

"Come on. There are rich guys all over who'd marry me in a minute. It's Johnson County, the Beverly Hills of the Heartland. You could roll a bowling ball down the street and trip up three or four rich guys. Well, not in my complex. Listen, I'm sure you could marry a poor girl if you want. There's scads of 'em around here, and some come equipped with bratty kids."

Feeling shame for having romanticized this icy woman, he mumbled, "Man, I'm such a dumb-ass. Why am I such a fool?"

Erin's voice softened. "Don't go there. You'll be fine. Ian's just different. So assertive."

"It's easy to be assertive when you're rich. People pay attention when you're rich."

"Look, this is going in circles and frankly I'm getting bored by it all. So, before I hang up, let me say you're a cute guy and a gentleman, and people might like you if they have the patience to. But what can I say? I just hope the three of us can all be friends."

The sounds of the shower got louder, which suggested she'd pulled the curtain and was ready to begin the cleansing process. He refused to picture her shower scrubby, pink or possibly blue, drooping below the nozzle like a corsage at midnight. He refused to see her jars and tubes of specialty oils and shampoos, off-brand all, but extravagances nonetheless. And he desperately refused to imagine her naked body—he shut his eyes with violence.

He said, "So I guess I won't drop by tonight after all."

"Yeah, you should go ahead and not drop by tonight."

"Cool. The three of us can all be friends together some other night."

Sunday the 14th

What happened at the happy hour was a downer, but the rest of Adam's story does not drip with drear. Neither will these pages sag with scenes of him punching pillows or heaving breakable heirlooms or writhing naked in the forest, his flesh painted red and black. Granted, Adam's world *was* wrecked. Though he'd had a couple-dozen dates with three or four women these past few years, Erin was the only one he'd ever taken seriously. So he did have to push hard to get through a few days. For a time he skipped work, skipped meals, and considered skipping his daily showers. He even did the things you've seen jilted guys do in the movies: on Thursday he sniffed an armpit of a shirt from his floor and concluded it was okay; on Friday he took three swallows of scotch straight from the bottle and wiped his mouth on his bare arm; on Saturday he watched infomercials back-to-back for stackable pots and pans. And all the while he relived key moments from that single date with Erin. *Let's make this a teachable experience*, he'd told himself in a brighter moment. By and by, things got a little less awful, and by the weekend he concluded Ian Moon might have done him a favor.

By Sunday he was ready to get on with his life, and so he planned to visit an indie coffee shop nearby. He'd take a book along to impress any women of substance there. After his shower, Adam surveyed the small shelf in his room. He weighed the implications of many spines and settled on *Daisy Miller*. He knew a little about it and thought it might send the right signals to a young woman of quality and discretion.

Soon he left his apartment, for the first time since the Wednesday call with Erin from the parking lot of Thirsty Mack's. He wondered if everything would look different, but everything in his suburban village looked exactly the same. He landed in a coffee shop in an older strip mall. Among the dozen customers, only one qualified as a young woman seated alone. Twelve feet away, in profile, she stared lifelessly into a laptop, her elbows on the tabletop, her palms atop her cheeks. Adam watched her for a long time, his nose poking above the book in a crocodilian pose. From this angle, she didn't seem bad—skinny and shapeless, maybe, with a pointy chin and short hair. The woman never looked his way, but when she finally moved her hands to the keyboard, he noticed a diamond ring decorating a certain finger.

So this is how it's gonna be, he said to himself.

Frustrated, he set *Daisy Miller* aside and reached for a tabloid that lay open. *Flagrance* was an alternative news-weekly of the sort that littered the shops, sidewalks, and recycling bins of every big city. It was targeted to artists and bohemians, but its pages of ads for escorts and dildos suggested it captured a corporate audience as well. Adam skimmed an article with the headline "Food and Shoes Are This Charity's Bread and Butter." It was about a reformed addict who'd founded a non-profit called "Loaves and Loafers." The caption identified him, carelessly, as the founder of "Loaves *for* Loafers." Adam wished he could start a charity so he could say good-bye to Teletech. He could spend his days helping people who genuinely needed it instead of making rich people richer. *I really have been the happiest when I've helped others*, he reminded himself. He made a mental note to give serious thought to the prospects of helping others more often, as soon as his life slowed down a little.

For now, he turned to the back for the Personals section. Amid all the sordid notices and lurid phone numbers, his eye got drawn to an item with the heading "Cheap Advice from a Rich Lady." He read the following:

What is up? I'm 35, smart, and filthy rich. My greatest wish is to "give back to the community." So I will offer my time in 30-minute sessions at just $5 each, during which I will give advice on topics of your choice. You may ask, "Why is a rich lady charging a fee?" The small sum will filter out those men who are lonesome, or seeking a wife, or just wishing to "feel me up." In other words, "Axe murderers need not apply!" Do I happen to be a licensed psychologist? No. But I am eager to lend an ear and share my real-world smarts. If you wish to buy a session, call 816-555-0907. We can meet in public so there is no "monkey business." By the way, I do carry a stun gun—fair warning.

Adam had half a mind to call this rich lady and salute her for giving back to the community. *Not all rich people are thugs, of course*, he reminded himself as he took the paper to the privacy of his car. The red Camry was parked in the sun because there was no shade as far as the eye could squint. He donned his sunglasses, powered up the A.C., and punched in the numbers. A woman answered.

"Uh, I thought I'd get a machine," he croaked. "I was gonna leave a nice message or maybe a prank one or . . . I don't even know."

"Who this?"

"Not an axe murderer?" he said hesitantly.

She groaned so powerfully that Adam felt the hairs in his ears flutter.

"How you get fooled by some dumb shit like that anyway? Dude, I am butt-ass broke and I don't be givin' no advice to nobody." Her voice was deep and smoky, more manly than sexy. "You see, there's this white boy that works at that paper which tried to take me out for a fish sammich, but I said no. And so he went and did this to me for revengeance. For real."

"Man. Sorry. I mean, I figured it might be a prank, the diction and all. Anyway, I bet your phone's ringin' off the hook."

"Only got one call so far."

"Just one?"

"Lady wanted to know should she be soakin' her chicken meat in salty water."

"Like, before you fry it?"

"That's right. I told her to give it a try. Ain't no skin off my ass."

After his self-imposed exile, Adam was pleased to have a civilized conversation again. "I suppose it couldn't hurt. Unless it made it too salty. But just one call was all you got?"

"My phone been busted up a while. So why'd *you* call me up?"

"Uh, maybe to see if this ad was for real. Maybe I felt like talking. Anyway, you see, I just lost my girlfriend and—"

"Kilt dead?"

"No, no. She was steppin' out on me."

"That ain't right."

"Hey, it *isn't* right. And, like, for a time I thought she was perfect for me. I was planning to marry her and live happily ever after."

"Now you be soundin' all cracker and shit."

"Sorry. You're right. You're right."

"Just go on with your story. Get to the good parts."

"Well, yes. I mean, the other day I learned she's been seeing this loser behind my back. Ian Moon. This dopey-lookin' con man who gets old people to sign up for expensive things they don't need."

"That ain't no way to treat folks."

"And he doesn't even need the money. Because he's already rich. *Born* rich, of course."

"Born with that silver spoon in his baby-ass mouth."

"Yes! Yes!"

"Sound to me like you're better off without her."

"For sure. Thank you. I mean, who could ever trust her again? She failed the biggest test there is for relationships, and it broke . . . oh this is all so weird. I never talk about stuff like this. It's all so boring. I'm truly sorry."

"Stop kickin' your ass in the ass. I like the stories you tell. So how 'bout lettin' the poor rich lady give you some cheap advice. First off, we gettin' along good here, but don't go fallin' in love with *me* now. I'm just a big ol' mean one myself. But if you do, the fool that wrote the ad, he'll get all jealous and write up one about you. He ain't much to look at, but he's mean. Ain't rich at all, workin' at that bullshit paper like that. But us ladies do like the rich guys. You probably ain't rich neither."

"Heck no," he said proudly.

"But you said the other one is? The crook? This Goober Star?"

"Ian Moon."

"Maybe that's all it is, baby. It ain't personal against you. It's only personal 'bout your wallet. That girl just likes the green. Do her nipples get stiff when she whiffs the cash?"

"I don't know," he replied, struggling to keep up.

"If you really wanna get her back, you need to get rich is all."

"Wait. Get her back? As in revenge or as in winning her back?"

"That be up to you. So either way, get yourself rich."

"The last thing the world needs is another rich guy."

"Why'd you call me up then if you didn't want my advice? All kindsa better stuff I could be doing right now."

"No, I mean, thanks, but it's complicated. For instance, my dad was this guy who—"

"Child, I got some pork butts on the fire, so just listen to me now. Hear this now: Go out and buy yourself a lottery ticket."

"A lottery ticket," he said, rolling his eyes. "Hmm. Well, super then. A lottery ticket. Super. You've given me a lot to think about. Right. Okay. So, thanks, Rich Lady. Yes, I've taken up enough of your time already. Should I mail you five bucks?"

"You be tryin' to get my street address?" She cackled a laugh. "Ha! I just knew you'd fall for me."

Friday the 19th

Adam Durham was employed in a satellite office for a global enterprise based in Houston whose mission was to acquire other concerns while itself being acquired by other concerns. The five-storey building stood tall between tiny ponds and sprawling parking lots in a corporate common in a Kansas City suburb. Any hopes the designers once had for a placid setting had long been scotched by the cacophony of lawn care equipment, skateboards, and high-strung ducks and geese. On the second floor, in a cubicle darkened by certificates, a woman read a document while Lori Nelson watched from a sidelong stance, one foot inside the cube, the other in the aisle. This Lori, rather compact at five-five, had a figure full of delightful curves. If you stretched those curves into a single line, it might reach halfway to Topeka. Her hair, Scandinavian-blonde, fell short of the shoulders of her slate-blue suit. Her eyes were blue, of course, and her brows visible only because of their thickness. Her mouth was small, and her top lip arched to a pouty point.

The supervisor swiveled and faced her guest. "So, Lori, today marks two full weeks here. It seems that things are going well."

"Very well." She nodded just once. Many in her spot would have nodded nonstop with the intent to convince, but Lori was comfortable in her own skin and also in the executive suit she'd chosen to wear on Casual Friday.

"Good. Good. Listen, I've noticed you've grasped our methods and procedures, which happens to be no small feat."

"They've been mapped very well. Very impressive." Then, to her own surprise, she got distracted by a guy crossing the nearest aisle. It was a rare lapse in discipline and she blushed because of it.

"You do not want to go there," directed the supervisor, her brows and lips long and squiggly, as if sketched by a cartoonist in a hurry.

"What?"

"Adam Durham. One of the malcontents," she whispered. "Pretty much a hermit. A rare sighting of the unhappy beast."

"Why should he be unhappy?" she whispered back, much the way a healthy person will whisper when speaking with a laryngitic.

The woman softly slapped her kneecap. "Thank you, Lori. That's what I'd like to know.'"

***

The second-floor break room at Teletech Tech was a numbing square, yellow to the eye and gray to the heart, its walls bald but for a few EEOC documents and handwritten reminders about "science experiments" that festered in the refrigerator. Burdening one table were two zucchini spears, late from someone's garden. Seated at a second table with their sack lunches were Adam's cube neighbors, Carlos Williams and Tyler Jones. Each fellow had shaggy hair and each wore glasses with rust-colored frames. Carlos was thin enough to alarm most grandmas, whereas Tyler was pasty and plump. For a year the two had been the best of friends in every wholesome way, a friendship grounded in their status as odd ducks at Teletech and beyond—at least that's how they saw it. Often in their isolated corner they'd swap the most gruesome self-deprecating remarks, which cracked them up. The two were in love. Platonic love, of course.

But each in his own innocent way might have loved Adam Durham even more.

The whole darn deal was complicated. They could tell Adam was an outsider like them, but only because he chose it. He *looked* like the sensible frat brother who speaks to the media whenever a pledge dies from overdosing on grain alcohol. But it went beyond his looks. They concluded he had the wit, the brains, and the social skills to stand out at Teletech or anyplace, but, bravely, he chose to lay low and excel only when he wanted.

Now the man was six feet away, staring into the vending machine. The guys would've given a pretty penny to know his private thoughts. They *were* aware that a woman named Erin had left him; days earlier, Trip from down the hall had noticed Adam's absences, had connected the dots, and had gone around the second floor whispering from the side of his mouth.

Now Adam turned. "Hey guys, what's the difference between that bag of Munchos in there and the three of us?"

The duo leaned for a better look. It turned out there were *two* slots that held Munchos.

"Which bag?" asked Tyler, pointing back and forth.

"It doesn't matter."

Tyler said, "Oh. Hmm, uh, they're inorganic and we aren't?"

"No-o-o," said Adam, stretching the word like a game show host pretending to be sympathetic. He looked at Carlos.

"Uh, they're crunchier? I mean, shoot, that was stupid. I don't know." He gave his forehead a soft slap.

Tyler said, "Is this a trick question? Because maybe there is no difference?"

"Yes! Good call, Tyler." He pointed at a tiny bag of Munchos and, like a prosecutor, vigorously said, "That bag of chips and the three of us are all trapped behind a glass facade, waiting for someone to free us."

His confidence boosted, Tyler chirped, "I know it. I mean, we *are* in a glass building, except for the girders and stuff."

Adam dropped his hands deep inside his pockets. "Sorry for pissing in your lunch buckets like this. I need to quit pouting. We've all got problems, don't we?"

The two boys nodded with vigor.

"But on top of everything else, work has really sucked extra today," said Adam. "I've got those PowerPoint blues again."

In a controlled squeal, Carlos said, "Why they insist on wasting your talents around here, it's so stupid."

Adam shrugged. "I'm sure they're wasting yours too. What is it you guys do again?" He gave a single clap. "Anyway, listen: I'm gonna step out for lunch. Can I trust you boys to behave while I'm gone?"

"Hey, I heard something interesting about the new girl," called Tyler.

In the doorway, Adam halted.

Carlos said, "Which new girl? Monique or that little blonde, Lori what's-her-name?"

Tyler said, "Monique, moron. Like he'd ever be interested in Lori."

"But Lori's hot," Carlos blurted impulsively. "I mean, but not really. I mean, she's a dog, right? A real bowser."

Adam chuckled from his short distance. "That little Lori is a piece of work. Too ambitious to wear jeans on Casual Friday." He came closer and lowered his voice. "I don't know her, but she might be the poster girl for everything I despise about the corporate world."

"Would it kill her to put on blue jeans?" asked Tyler, his arms outstretched in the fashion of an exasperated basketball coach.

"Hey, Adam, you moved in on Monique yet?"

In the brief time since his break-up with Erin, Adam had twice joked with the boys about whisking the leggy Monique to a weekend hideaway, but that's all it was: joking. After all, the woman was engaged to be married and he was not the type of guy to complicate a thing like that.

"You guys know I can't."

Tyler was happy to break some news. "Right, but according to my sources, it turns out she *used to be* engaged. It turns out the guy decided he was gay."

"Really?" said Adam, coming one step closer.

Carlos laughed. "Sources. Ha! Like you've got sources. He just means Drowsy Todd."

"The CFO?" said Adam. "Tyler, why are you chatting with the CFO?"

"No, Drowsy Todd's the janitor. With the beer gut," answered Carlos, forming a phantom paunch with his palms.

"You ever talk to her?" asked Tyler.

With a bashful grin, Adam said, "Oh, you know. We've smiled at each other in the aisles and said 'hi' a few times. She kind of titters when she says 'hi.' I like that. Bashful people don't get enough credit in this world." He then slapped the doorframe as if to knock "good bye."

When Adam was gone, Carlos said, "Bro, if he and Monique hook up, we'll never get to hang with him. He's so private, and she's so bashful, they'll never go out in public."

"Oh I'm afraid they'll hook up," warned Tyler. "I mean, it's Adam we're talking about. Why in the world wouldn't she?"

***

During the lunch rush at Brody's Quick Shop, Adam gripped his yogurt in one hand and his banana in the other and stared at a flashing message for the Heartland Lucky Six lottery. According to the sign, the drawing would be held tonight and the jackpot was higher than $5 million—a lot higher if the number of exclamation points was indicative of the sum. He chuckled as he remembered the rich lady's silly advice from a week or so ago. But he also had half a mind to call her again, just to catch up and rap about stuff. Ahead of him, a geezer in a fedora hat bought a stack of lottery tickets. As he left the counter, they unfurled in his hand like a paper accordion. His wife tried to snatch them. He pulled away.

"Sign those tickets fast," she snarled.

Grumbling, the old man shook her off and hobbled to the door. Adam had a spasm of fear that he, too, would end up like that old couple someday if he wasn't careful – especially if he settled on the wrong partner.

With the change from his five-spot, he flipped a buck to the clerk and said, "Hell, I never do this, but one Heartland ticket. Because a very wise rich lady insisted I buy one."

Awhirl in his duties, the clerk said, "Gee, that is so interesting."

Ignoring the sarcasm, Adam slipped the ticket into the left-side back pocket of his blue jeans, where it would be safe.

***

The clock numbers flickered large on Adam's desktop monitor and he didn't care who in management might walk past and spot them. He watched the digits crawl closer and closer to closing time. In contrast, his visitors, Carlos and Tyler, feared the numbers were advancing too fast! On Fridays the duo always dropped by Adam's at this late hour, hoping to insinuate themselves into his weekend plans. They hadn't been successful yet, but things were different now. Adam was single again. Plus, a nice guy from the third floor was throwing a pool party that night and the whole building was invited.

Carlos put it all on the line. "I just wanna clock outta here and get to Luke's party." He knew Adam wouldn't normally bother with a work party, so his voice sweetened with this sweet news: "There's gonna be two kegs."

The citation of two kegs did nothing to quicken Adam's pulse. It was doubtful *two hundred* kegs would stir him.

"It could be a trip. The party, I mean," Carlos followed.

Adam didn't wish to fritter a single minute at a Teletech pool party, but he also sensed these two boys would never attend without him, and it was clear they wanted to go. Perhaps performing a good deed would cheer him up.

"I hear Monique's going," blurted Tyler. "Hey, Adam, in a swimming pool the rules of the road are different. You can get away with all kinds of naughty horseplay. At least, I bet you can." He leaned closer and whispered, "How'd you like her lovely wet legs to straddle your neck?"

With his feet crossed on his desktop, his hands in his lap, and his lips set in an understated curl, Adam came to a quick conclusion. "I mean, what the hell. Maybe I will go. See how the other half lives for a change."

Carlos and Tyler folded as if coiling for a victory leap, and though they didn't leap, they did spring upright and attained more altitude by throwing fists of joy.

Tyler said, "Adam, man, this is your lucky day. First off, seeing Monique in those tight-fittin' jeans around here. And tonight, Monique in a hot bikini I bet."

Adam dropped his feet to the floor and placed his fingers on the keyboard to log out for the week. Coolly, for the amusement of his pals, he said, "And tomorrow morning, as the sun peeks through my blinds, Monique in nothing but my bed."

***

Thanks to low interest rates and a sluggish market, Luke from the third floor was able to buy a nice house in a subdivision not far from Teletech. He was drawn to the property because of its wet bar and its in-ground pool, which would open up his social life and perhaps get him into decent physical shape before his next high school reunion.

When Adam and his two colleagues arrived in their three-car procession, it was still eighty-five degrees. The late-summer sun slanted upon two women who lazed on inflatable rafts in the pool, sometimes drifting into the lane of an older man with silvery chest hair who strode very deliberate laps, his expression bleak. Several other Teletech guests lounged in patio chairs or mingled on the deck, some of them sometimes laughing louder than necessary.

Through the gate, the boys followed Adam straight to the kegs. His goal for this naked beeline was to avoid making eye contact, which was the same goal he had at the office every day. At the kegs, a shrimpy guy from the IT department offered a lesson on how best to pump the keg and tilt the cup for minimal foam. After two perfect demonstrations, he freed the tap and threw up his arms as if to say *I'm just one man; it's in your hands now*. After Adam and the boys poured their own beers, they unstacked some chairs and placed them at the near end, beneath the shade of a tree. Adam pulled his wadded trunks from a pocket and put them on his lap. He decreed they would stay dry until Monique got wet.

Seeing the swimming trunks, Tyler said, "I'd have brought mine, except I'm too fat."

"I've got these pelican legs," said Carlos, pointing at a knee.

"You guys could skinny dip."

Carlos laughed.

Tyler laughed. "Ha. No way. You think?"

Adam looked at the entrance gate, which was past the tiny pool house about fifty feet away. Near that pool house, the host and a buddy were executing a most elaborate handshake.

"This is starting to suck. Where the hell is that Monique?"

"Yeah," said Tyler. "Where the hell is she already?"

And then, as if on cue, the gate creaked! The three rose just enough and stretched just enough for a better view.

"Hey, that's not Monique," Adam said, lowering.

"Not even," confirmed Carlos.

Instead, crossing that narrow entrance was the dreaded Lori Nelson, the other new girl from work, the ambitious blonde who was too damn good for Casual Friday.

"What happened to her business suit?" quipped Adam.

Indeed, she was not overdressed for *this* occasion. Lori wore a tee-shirt that reached the knees, which, owing to her height, was not that far to reach. This light-blue top obscured whatever swimwear might lie beneath it. Trailing the unsmiling blonde was a burly, balding, blunt-faced bloke on the dark side of his thirties, in khakis, polo, and loafers. His steely expression and general demeanor suggested he could be Lori's bodyguard or else her mean dad. He clutched a designer gym bag and surveyed the scene from north to south with one scornful swipe of the eyes. Then those same eyes fixed on the kegs and stayed there a long moment. He urged Lori toward the stockade of beer and then went deeper into the action, eventually placing his gym bag on the first table in his path, which happened to be near Adam, Carlos, and Tyler. He extended a hand and waited for any of them to rise and shake it.

"Mike Smith," he announced triumphantly, as if the citation of his name was somehow rubbing it in.

Hands were duly shaken and feeble introductions were duly made and duly forgotten, after which he sat on a corner of the table and squinted at the pool until Lori returned with two plastic cups of beer. She gave one to her date, who proceeded to complain about the excess foam and then about having left his new sunglasses in the car, parked half a block away.

Made nervous by the fellow's presence, Tyler soon squeaked, "So, what do you do?"

Mike Smith turned his head, his eyes a-squint. "I'm an entrepreneur. A self-made man, yeah. It's all good. Can't complain."

"Good for you," Carlos said. "You're lucky."

"Luck's got nuttin to do with it, boys," he said.

What he didn't say was he inherited a sizable sum from his father, who'd held a murky position in finance before dying from a massive coronary eighteen months ago, just days before a federal indictment was to be served. Before that tragedy, Mike Smith had never been consistently employed, and now in possession of his late father's loot he had no reason to be.

"Well, what I mean is, we all hate our jobs. Us three, anyway."

In truth, Carlos didn't hate his job, and neither did Tyler. After all, Teletech paid them to hang out together in a climate-controlled setting, with a break room, vending machines, foosball in the basement, and clean restrooms nearby. But Carlos was having fun at the poolside, and he hoped the lie would impress Adam and keep him there longer, at least until Monique arrived, if she arrived.

"You guys hate your jobs? My advice: quit," said Mike Smith.

Adam took a drink and looked the other way. He wished his neck made noise so everyone in that back yard would know he had *chosen* to look the other way.

"I actually bought a lottery ticket today," blurted Carlos.

"Won't catch me wasting a buck like that until the return gets high enough," claimed Mike Smith.

"Five or six million isn't high enough?"

The thick man tilted his chin and laughed.

Adam could no longer resist. "Shoot, man, if I had just twenty-five grand, I'd quit my job and not work again for a long, long time."

"And let your 401K stall out?" asked Lori, who peeked from behind her escort.

"Twenty-five large? Chicken change," scoffed Mike Smith.

Now beside him, Lori arched her brows and started stepping away.

With a tone of finality, the big guy put it all into simple-speak: "I do well because so many guys got their thumb up their ass."

The loathsome phrase *chicken change* made Adam very eager to leave. But as he began the tricky process of rising from a rickety folding chair while clutching a cup of beer in one fist and swimming trunks in another, the entrance gate creaked! That gate flung open and the heavens delivered a long-legged vision in a tee-shirt sheer enough to tease the ghost of the black bikini beneath it. This solo guest was very tan, with full brows and layered brown hair that fanned past her shoulders. In the movies such an entrance might be captured in slow-motion, with careful angles and careful lighting, backed by a soundtrack heavy with the lightness of strings. But this entrance was grand without those special effects because Monique was singularly beautiful. And to Adam's eye she was made more darling by her shyness. The woman moved tentatively—even *clumsily*—as she hunched her shoulders and looked all around, her eyes seeking the eyes of the host or any comforting face. It was so cute, so genuine! Adam just grinned and grinned as if the story's happy ending was already written. Yes, Monique might be the reward for the heartbreak he'd just been through. Maybe he *would* whisk her to a weekend hideaway. Though far apart, this man and this woman locked eyes, and Adam was certain her right brow leapt, as if to say *Good, you are here*. *You are here*.

Adam planned to go after it! So far in life he'd always neglected such opportunities because he'd worried about public humiliation, but now he realized it was stupid to care about what people that you didn't like thought of you. So, yes, by God, he would meet her halfway, show her the trunks, and say something clever.

With little commotion he got himself out of that flimsy chair and onto his sneakers. But at that same moment, for crying out loud, Mike Smith lifted his goddamn flanks from the tabletop nearby, which sent the table bouncing, which upset some beers, which sent the big man burling into Adam's path as he dashed to dodge the splashes. Brief as they were, these events slowed Adam's progress just enough, just enough, and by the time he worked his way around Mike Smith's torso, he saw Luke hugging Monique in the way only the party host can get away with.

Knowing Luke didn't have a prayer with this beauty, Adam announced to his friends he was ready to take a friendly dip. Carlos nodded. Tyler gave a thumbs-up sign. These were two chaps who knew the score.

He started for the pool house. The brawny Mike Smith caught up and gave him a knowing elbow to the ribs. "Need to practice my breast-stroke, if you catch my drift."

Inside the pool house—a cobwebby tool shed, really—the men made the most of their small distance as they disrobed. Adam did not dare to bare his ass and was grateful to observe, accidentally, that Mike Smith retained his own skivvies beneath his own swim trunks as well. He watched the older man cram his clothes into a gym bag, which sat safely on a wooden stool, above all the mess.

"That dude Luke should've straightened this place out," Adam mumbled as he sought a place to secure his jeans. He thought about taking them back to his chair poolside, but that would've felt weird. There were probably some garments you could carry around at a party, but blue jeans did not qualify. He held the wadded denims with both hands and went "Hmm."

"What?" said Mike Smith, annoyed.

"You mind if I set these jeans on top of your bag? So they don't get infested with mildew and rats and stuff on the floor there."

Making for the exit, the big guy shrugged. "Whatever tickles your tits."

"I think I'll take my valuables though." He salvaged his wallet and keys before dropping the wadded jeans on the top of the unzipped bag.

Outside, Adam halted upon seeing a horrible sight within that water: Monique was straddling someone else's shoulders—the shoulders of a Van Halen roadie!

Truth be told, the guy might not have been a Van Halen roadie, but the odds were in its favor. He had a mane of feathered hair that was too inky for his advanced age. His bony face was a road map of wrinkles. His arms and chest were like those of a starving child's, except for the tattoos, which at this late date resembled Rorschach blots that had been folded and spindled by too many sweaty fingers over the years.

Carlos was kind enough to answer Adam's unspoken question: "Uh, that would be Trevor, Luke's ex-brother-in-law. He lives here too, but just until his luck changes."

"I think it has," Adam said.

***

For unknown reasons, sometimes ballplayers on the losing team will slump in the dugout and watch the champions celebrate around the pitchers' mound long after the final out in the World Series has been recorded. In a similar way, Adam watched Trevor and Monique enjoy a variety of ass-grabbery games in and upon the water. The shy brunette, no longer constrained by that marriage engagement, giggled and shrieked while her mirthful partner delivered his signature phrase: "Now that's just aces."

Actually, Adam felt no heartbreak. Not this time. For one, he was bored with the grips of sadness. More so, he hadn't invested much spiritual energy into the *ideal* of Monique; she'd only been a diversion and only for a short while. His loss amounted to the loss of a weekend of debauchery.

Soon he turned to Tyler. "So, what's this Trevor have anyway?"

"I think it's confidence. You should've seen him go straight up and sweet-talk her when you were in there changing. Women eat up that shit. Confidence, I mean."

“Good call,” said Adam. “It is shit. You know who else was confident? General Custer was confident. So was Bobby Riggs. And you can go ahead and put Ian Moon in that God-damned group, I’d say.”

Adam rose and with a heavy step made for the keg.

“Ian Moon?” Tyler asked, leaning across the empty chair.

Carlos nodded. “The fifth Beatle, dummy. Jumped out a hotel window and got replaced by Ringo.”

***

The intrusion of this tattooed Trevor did Mike Smith no favors either. There is no delicate way to put it: He hated guys like Trevor. He hated guys like Trevor even when they weren’t romping with women like Monique, whom he also hated, mostly because she was a woman. Bottom line—the whole thing made him want to puke. Instead, he went into the kitchen in his trunks, seeking cake. Minutes later, he and Lori emerged in a spat that got more intense with each step taken. He followed her poolside, where they continued bickering in measured volumes. Even as he argued, Mike Smith poked tall stacks of Pringles into his mouth.

He said, “Come on. Get some hair on your nuts. It was a harmless joke.”

“Not to a Korean it wasn’t.”

“Screw ‘em if they can’t take a joke in my country.”

“He’s one of my directors, for God’s sake!”

“He can kiss my ass,” he asserted through a mouth full of chips.

Lori put her hands on her hips and tilted her head. “Seriously? What was I ever thinking? Just shoot me, someone.”

Mike Smith clapped sarcastically, and with nine pairs of eyes upon him he performed a wooden pirouette and said, “Hey, we got a comedian here. It’s Whoopi Goldberg, everyone!”

Lori backed away. Her mouth grinned but her eyes resisted. Quietly, she said, “Is this really happening?” She looked from face to embarrassed face before placing her hands on either side of her head and laughing derisively. She then made for a bank of empty chairs on the opposite end. Meanwhile, Mike Smith swiped the Pringles’ dust from his hands as he strode to the pool house, where his designer bag awaited.

Carlos said, “Geez, you almost feel sorry for her.”

Adam shrugged. “But that’s the risk you take when you go out with rich guys.”

In another corner, Monique was splayed in a lounge chair that was rusty, blotched, and frayed, much like Trevor himself, who knelt on a towel beside her and recited amusing things. Adam gazed passively in that direction for two or three minutes, oblivious to the mutterings of those nearby who were reliving the highlights of the spat between Lori Nelson and Mike Smith. Indeed, he was bored with the merry couple across the way, and with the panting chatter all around him, and with the subpar chairs and the bare male dugs and the hairy armpits and the knobby knees and the fishbelly-white paunches and everything else and everyone else, and so he bid a quiet good-bye to Carlos and Tyler with a pistol-finger salute.

"You're going?" they asked in unison.

He responded with a second, more listless, pistol-finger salute. Next, he reached to the table for his keys and wallet before heading to the pool house. A minute later he emerged from that pool house and went straight to where Lori sat. She was visiting with a Teletech intern named Holly.

He leaned low and said, "Excuse me. Lori? I'm Adam Durham. Second floor. Technical Synergies. Listen, I hate to butt in. Long story short, my jeans just happened to be in that Mike Smith guy's gym bag."

"What?" Clearly, this Lori was not pleased to be reminded of that guy.

"Yeah. I know it sounds weird, but it's totally innocent how they got there, I'm sure. I mean, I'm not calling the guy a thief or anything."

"Oh you can call him anything," she said.

"Right."

Earlier, Lori had shed the light-blue shirt, which left her in the one-piece swimsuit, and from this aerial angle Adam got a full serving of her cleavage. He'd never been much of a breast man—*you can see boobs on fat men at the beach*, he often said, though he'd never been near a beach—but suddenly his universe was shifting; her cleavage was that provocative! To put things in their proper historical perspective, the three pairs of breasts he'd so far had privileges with in life had all been flawed. One pair was too mammoth to take seriously; he sort of batted at them like inflatables in a fast-food playroom. The second pair was too conical, drooping like jesters' caps. And the third set was composed largely of polyurethane. But, man, these jubblies of Lori's, so cozy within that one-piece—

"Adam? Adam? Hey, I said he's gone. The bad man with your pants is gone. What do you expect me to do?"

"Oh! Sorry! Hey, uhm, I don't know," he stammered. "I mean, yeah, they must have fallen in his bag in that pool shed. My jeans, I mean. It was kinda dark in there by the time he left, so I guess he didn't see 'em."

"Okay," she said, dragging out the second syllable to show derision, mostly for the benefit of Holly the intern. "Are there any valuables in the pockets? Your keys, for instance? Cash money? A turtle dove?"

He smiled. He did not like her, of course, but he liked her rack and he loved the "turtle dove" line. He said, "I guess maybe you can give me his phone number, if you don't mind."

"Usually men ask me for *my* number."

"I'm sure they do."

Lori gave her leg a slap as if to bring things to a speedy conclusion, like whipping a horse in a race. "Well, I do have his cell number if you really want it. Yes, the man's number has gone and polluted my phone. So I'm gonna have to flush it down the toilet here pretty soon."

I've got a live wire here, he told himself, and he grinned, mostly for the benefit of Holly the intern.

"But you're welcome to call him," she added, still heated up from that public spat. "It's a free country. Me, I never want to speak to the bastard again."

Adam could not have known he was pondering the biggest decision of his life so far. Had he stuck to his guns and asked again for the number, the story could end right here. Instead, he stroked his chin as he pictured the process of tapping out the digits on his phone and then explaining things to the brawny Mike Smith.

He said, "On second thought, they're just jeans. Gettin' a little ragged around the cuffs, you know. So, yeah, thanks anyway." And he gave a pistol-finger good-bye, mostly for the benefit of Holly the intern.

The two women watched him go.

Lori said, "What a sad sack."

"He didn't seem sad to me."

"No. I can sense these things. He's . . . troubled."

"Well, his girlfriend just ditched him for some rich guy," said Holly the intern.

"How do you know?"

"You haven't heard? It's been sort of mildly big news around the office."

"Mildly big news? Him? Who the hell cares?"

"You'd be surprised. He's a very nice guy. He was really helpful to me one time, and I'm just a chubby intern."

Lori made a "tsk" sound, but soon added this: "A rich guy, you say? She left him for a rich guy. Well, I'm sure the woman had her reasons."

"I don't know. I think he's kinda cute. Those lashes."

"Well lashes ain't everything, sister."

Holly the intern swiveled her upper body and affected a strained smile. She said, "Lori, I've never seen you like this. So . . . tart and blunt and all."

"Well, yeah," she said, glumly. "I just get this way sometimes. Only when I'm mad at myself."

***

Near the northern end of this same sprawling suburb of Kansas City, most of the homes were small bungalows that dated all the way back to the 1970s, and most had single-car garages, tiny lawns, and front-porch slabs just big enough to accommodate a Smoky Joe grill and a large cat. Inside each house, one might also find the sensation of a troubling smallness, as if the boxy homes had been carved into too many rooms in an effort to tease away that very sensation of smallness.

On the Friday night of the dismal pool party, Scotty O'Connor reclined in an easy chair in the living room of one such bungalow and stared at a college football game with the face of a fan whose team was getting creamed. But this football game was not fueling his frown. Finances were. And injustice. And even pride.

Scotty was a fat, freckled guy who always wore sweats, jerseys, and ball caps, perhaps because he never went anywhere that called for better dress. He was the type of guy the zany beer commercials were targeted to. In those ads, the babes often found the oafs like him to be sweet and endearing, but in the real world no babe had ever given this poor guy a glance that didn't contain contempt, pity, indifference, or fear. Though an optimist, at thirty-two he was starting to think he'd never score such a babe—or much of any woman, and so increasingly the beer ads and the supermodels saddened him. But at least he had his freedom; nobody could tell him what to do. Except, if you wanted to get technical, you could say he answered to his housemate and business partner Fabrizio Leone, even though Fabrizio was four years younger and a half-foot smaller. The two had been inseparable since meeting five years ago while clerking at the Sneaker Grotto in the older mall.

The living room they rented was dark and cluttered with the debris of bachelors who ran a tiny bookmaking operation: PCs, beer cans, newspapers, chalkboards, mousetraps, jerseys, and miniature football helmets that once contained ice-cream sundaes. Its front door swung open and the housemate, Fabrizio, stepped in. He was a swarthy runt with narrow, rat-like eyes and thin black hair that ran too long on the sides. He was dressed in his typical style, like a grunge rocker who'd spiffed up for a charity event the night before, gotten madly drunk on free booze, crashed on somebody's couch, awakened in those same grungy clothes, and filched a purple stocking cap from the closet for the chilly walk home.

"Hear anything from our friend?" he asked even before he could shut the door. His voice was nasal and pinched, like those that on radio commercials that are meant to be wry. "Tell me you heard something."

"Our friend?"

"Mike Smith, you dumb-ass."

"He ain't our friend, and he ain't answering his phone still," replied Scotty. His voice, as always, was wheezy and phlegmatic. Though Fabrizio was the Italian with ancestors from Sicily, it was the Irishman Scotty who sounded Mafioso.

Fabrizio glared at him. He often glared at Scotty, sometimes for no reason. "Hey, we're gonna have to spook this bastard."

"I know it. But how?"

"We gotta get creative. We're smarter than him. Gotta think outside the box, you know."

Scotty gave a single clap, which marked a spike in his spirit. "Oh, how's this for thinkin' outside the box? I bought one of them lottery tickets today, when I was out south gettin' that Brody's mac-and-cheese I love – you know, the stuff they fix on the premise there, with the pizzas and the nachos and all. So I guess there's *some* hope for us no matter what. Six million, I think it is."

Still beside the door, as if going farther inside his own home would signal a commitment he was not prepared to make, Fabrizio said, "Hallelujah! A lottery ticket. Remind me to wipe my ass on it later."

"People win those things all the time. You've seen the news."

"Scotty, the choices you make. Lottery ticket? Come on. You know I can replace you in five minutes."

Scotty gazed into his orb of a lap. He had half a mind to tell his friend that he too could be replaced in five minutes, but it would be a lie, and Fabrizio would know it was a lie. They both knew that Fabrizio Leones did not grow on trees.

"Five minutes," the twerp repeated, displaying four fingers and a thumb.

"Why do you keep saying that, Fobb? It creeps me out. I thought we were equal partners."

With that same hand, Fabrizio gave a dismissive wave. "Hey, some people are more equal than others."

The comment *was* disdainful, as intended, but Fabrizio did have grounds for implying their match was uneven, at least on an intellectual level. While in high school he'd had a stepfather who was bright. The man, now off somewhere in Oregon with a different wife, had taught a general business course at the junior college, and in his free time he read some weekly magazines as well as books on all sorts of interesting topics, including history and the arts. While it's true that Fabrizio and this stepfather had never spoken beyond clipped remarks in passing, he did pick up heaps of knowledge because the stepfather talked loudly about contemporary matters while on the phone with friends. In contrast, Scotty had never known a father or a stepfather, and his mother was just a motel maid who never read a book.

Scotty's reply came in a soft whine: "But we been through a lot together, Fobb. At the store and all. Remember the good times? We had the secret hiding place. Nobody ever found us there, not even after we told 'em where it was."

Fabrizio came deeper into the dark room, which suggested he was warming up to something. "Ahh, hush it up for a while," he said, more gently. "You. Always livin' in the past." He fell back upon the couch and let his shrimpy legs dangle over its arm. He pulled the purple stocking cap over his eyes to make the darkness darker. "God how I wish Lenny Buck was still a bad guy. We could use his skills right now. What a simple answer to our problems. He'd take care of that Mike Smith for us. Get us our dough lickety split. But ever since he met that chick Ruthie, he's gone prissy on us."

"They say she made him learn to read," said Scotty.

"It's just another bullshit rumor! Anyway, so help me think outside the box on how we can we put ol' Lenny Buck on the bad-guy path once again."

"Wouldn't Ruthie just kick our ass?"

***

On the far-south side of town, in a newer subdivision of mansions, fountains, walking trails, wide roads, and wider roads, a Porsche 911 sped into the center of a three-car garage. Behind the wheel was Mike Smith, a big guy in a little car, returning alone from his maddening date with Lori Nelson. Though dusk was descending, he wore high-end sunglasses that made him look like a U.S. Secret Serviceman—at least, he was pretty sure they did. Well, maybe not so much at the moment on account of the trunks and flip-flips he also wore. Though expensive, the sunglasses always did one thing they were not advertised to do: they obscured his vision just a little by muting colors and contrasts. On this trip, for instance, he hadn't noticed the pair of denims that with each bump in the road dangled more and more from the dark gym bag that rode unzipped on the dark passenger seat.

In his garage, as he turned off the engine his cell phone rang. Mike Smith glanced at the caller ID and snapped the phone shut. He grabbed for his gym bag, but its strap got tangled in the stick shift. As he madly tried to free it, the bag flipped on its side and Adam's blue jeans spilled onto the dark floorboard. Mike Smith sat back down for the sake of leverage and then used both hands to dislodge the strap and free that damn bag. Next he slammed his door and grumbled some of swear words. He was in a hurry to get inside and open a cold beer and check out what cable had to offer. Friday nights were the best for cable porn, especially girl on girl, including, quite often, Asians.

Saturday the 20th

The next day, a lovely midwestern Saturday in the latest days of summer proper, a certain living room was as dim as dusk, as was the mood. In his recliner, Scotty O'Connor stared at a college football game, his lids drooping to half-mast. Crowding his lap were two remotes, his cell phone, the household landline, and a bag of Skittles. Suddenly the front door swept open, prosecuting the room with light. Fabrizio's silhouette, small as it was, darkened the doorway. In each hand sagged a sack from Dairy Queen. Just as quickly the room gloomed again as the door clicked shut.

"Ah, brazier burgers," Scotty said.

"At least we can enjoy that," grumped Fabrizio as he passed by with the sacks. "At least 'til we go tits-up and broke. Which we already are."

Scotty rose to meet the meal. "Texas-USC right now. And the Chiefs-Raiders tomorrow. And we're shut down here, Fobb. Is this any way to run a book?"

"Your tone of voice, it sounds like you're blaming me."

"I'm not blaming you. It's a lotta things. But mostly that Mike Smith guy. A stranger, and we go and let him bet real big like that. Over and over with no collateral."

"He ain't the only one that took us for fools."

"Well, right. Lotsa guys have, for too long now. But he's the worst."

Fabrizio went to the sunken section in the middle of the couch and unwrapped his chili dog. "We just gotta get our cash from him. That'll get us back on our feet. Cash flow is king."

Scotty returned to the easy chair with his lunch and a bottle of beer.

Fabrizio said, "Listen, you make any progress on my idea?"

The portly fellow was so pleased with his progress, he made the sacrifice of delaying his first bite to describe it all. "More I think about your idea, the more I like it. So we don't wanna kill the guy because then we don't get a dime outta him. Right? And so we don't wanna rough him up because we're basically not beasts. Right? But scare the sucker shitless, now that's something we can do."

"So now that you've wasted my time with things I already know, what you got for me?"

Grinning, Scotty leaned and reached and reached until his butt crack was publicized, serving rather like an exclamation mark to show his excitement. He then leaned back and handed over a page torn from an old Sports Illustrated. It was an action shot of former Oakland Raider Jack Tatum tackling a receiver from the New York Jets.

Fabrizio pumped some fries into his mouth and looked sidelong at the half-sheet. He turned it every which way. "Jack Tatum?"

Lustily, Scotty said, "The Assassin."

"What the hell?"

"I had to rip it off from the libarry. In the basement there, where they put all the dusty shit. Man, I dug and dug through a buttload of shit."

"You tore this outta the magazine there?"

Scotty nodded. "I mean, I don't like to tear up stuff from the libarry. But I pay my taxes."

"You ain't paid taxes since Sneaker Grotto! And you go and do this!"

"Sorry," he said, dragging out the word.

"Public property, Scotty! I have to live in this city too! Ah, anyways, you really think that's a good way to scare him? That we slap this on his windshield? Jack Freakin' Tatum?"

"The Assassin. Right? That was his nickname. Mike Smith sees this and he knows we're comin' after him, like assassins and all. You get it?"

"Sure I get it. But what you're doin' is what the perfessors call an allegory. Mike Smith wouldn't know an allegory if it chewed on his droopy nuts." As he spoke, the man's chili dog was held chin high, east to west, as if he was in a TV spot for chili dogs. He finally took a small bite of the frank, leaned back, and continued. "This guy's a dumbshit. He's just gonna think it's weird. Jack Tatum. Some washed-up clown from the sixties with a corny nickname. Look, he'll probably just figure some retarded kid put it on his car. Every block's got a retarded kid."

"We had one. Mitchell Lavender was his name. Called him 'Lav. He could not stop kissin' his mother."

"Fact is, you did not address the task I gave. Which was to go online and find pictures of some gruesome mob hits to scare the man. Albert Anastasia. Or Galante, with the cigar in his mouth. Big Paul."

"But that dial-up takes forever. I swear, by the time you see J-Lo's tit, she's went and got married again."

Fabrizio crumpled the page and threw it toward the kitchen. "Aw, we don't even know where the fucker lives. How can we put anything on his windshield when we can't even locate his windshield?"

"At least we got both his phone numbers. Home and cell." Scotty pointed south with a thumb. "And the first three numbers of his home line tell us he lives out in the southland."

"Like I said last night, that just narrows it to ten square miles. Hoo-rah."

"Did you ever look for it in the phone book?"

"Wadn't there. Jag-off could be unlisted."

"Did you try to track it down from the internet?"

"I tried this morning. Tried both numbers. But that shit don't work. The internet? Ha! What a joke that turned out to be."

***

By the dinner hour, Adam felt the need to get out of his apartment for a while. He figured Erin Patterson was out with Ian Moon, plotting ways to deceive seniors of their Medicare, and he figured Monique was out with Trevor, helping to put his tattoos back together. So Adam decided to make good use of his Saturday night as well by replacing the lost jeans. In a department store, with a new pair of denims slung over one shoulder, he strayed into Electronics. He was not interested in the latest cool gadgetry but was drawn to the big television screens because a local news anchor was especially gorgeous. He came closer and closer to the closest TV screen until he was close enough to kiss her pixilated lips. This lovely anchor happened to place the following news precisely into Adam's ear: "Closer to home, it looks like someone in our community is six million dollars richer after winning the Heartland Lottery last night. Yes, the lucky ticket was sold during the lunch hour yesterday at the Brody's Quick Shop on Quincy Avenue."

"Brody's!" Suddenly he needed space. He needed air. He backed away.

"Folks, check your tickets now because no one has stepped forward to claim the big prize. But, no real rush," she added. "The lucky winner has one year to come forward."

He draped the jeans on the nearest TV, grabbed his gut, and raced in the direction of the men's room.

***

Not far from that department store, in a gray and beige apartment within a beige and gray complex, slim Carlos Williams of Teletech phoned his best friend, the pudgy and pasty Tyler Jones, who was lying on his couch in his own gray apartment, pondering ways to make the Hostess Snowball in his hand last a little longer.

"Hey, Ty Ty, it's Saturday night. Time to go wild, my friend. What do you think?"

As they'd done on many weekend evenings, the two men volleyed the names of the hottest affordable hot spots in the southern suburbs. Tyler began with Maggie Q, his own piece of shorthand for The Magnificent Quaff.

"Love it. Except now they do karaoke on Saturday nights, and I bet that just brings in a lotta lonely old ladies."

"We can only hope," said Tyler.

"Ha! True. But we'd also be up against a lotta lonely old men with real money in their pockets. So, maybe we try Ethel's?"

"That's been taken over by kids' soccer teams. You know. Pizza parties. Soccer moms. Hey, wait a minute. Soccer moms!"

"Yeah, I like soccer moms," Carlos said hesitantly.

"But?"

"But there's a lotta soccer dads out there too. And they own guns."

"Well, then I guess there's always Snickers," Tyler suggested.

"Love it. Except, now they got a cover charge because they do improv on weekends."

"Snickers does improv? Man, now I've heard everything. I mean, just when you think you've heard it all."

Carlos nodded, even though he was on the phone. "Yeah, my cousin Jason went. The one that almost got drafted by the Redskins. He said all the actors kept pretending to be gay. I mean, it was hilarious at first but then it got old."

"So, I guess that leaves Thirsty's."

"Yes, Thirsty Mack's," Carlos confirmed. "Where the beer is hot and the women are ice cold! Ha!"

Tyler's voice quavered when he said, "You think Adam might go if we asked?"

"Don't get mad, Bro, but I already called. Twice, actually. No answer."

"Yeah. No surprise. He slummed with us last night. He's probably out doing something really cool right now to make up for it."

***

Bent over his kitchen table, Adam fingered through the white pages with fingers that trembled. He saw column after column of M Smiths, Michael Smiths, Micheal Smiths, Mike Smiths, plus a few Mikey Smiths which really pissed him off. Beyond that, he didn't even know what he was looking for. Frustrated, he slapped the directory shut. But he quickly reopened it and fluffed through some pages until he found a listing to his liking.

In her kitchen not far away, Lori's filtered voice echoed through the empty room: "Hi there. It's Lori. Please leave a concise message and have a super day."

In a shaky voice, like that of an old lady calling the cops, he left the following message: "Lori. Hey, this is Adam Durham from work. We talked last night at that party. Technical Synergies, second floor and all. Your friend or whatever took my jeans home. So, anyway, after much thinking and deliberation I'd like to get 'em back after all. So call me please at 913-555-2355. And hurry!"

***

Not that anyone ever asked him about it, but Mike Smith refused to call his basement a "man cave" because of the bad associations with the word "cave." Yet the space probably would qualify as a man cave. It was of a dark décor and sparsely appointed with a sectional couch, a coffee table, and a compact refrigerator. Of course, the basement had a very-big-screen TV as well. From the couch he navigated his remote control with one hand while scooping corn chips straight from the bag with the other. With his palm cupped sidelong at his mouth, like TV cowboys drinking from a stream, he devoured the snack chips with the gusto he typically reserved for red meat served rare. His tee-shirt and the crotch of his sweatpants were littered with shards, orts, crumbs, and corn dust. On the table beside him, the landline phone rang. He swiped his hand on his thighs and checked the caller ID. Defiantly, he placed the phone back on its dock. The call went to his answering machine:

"You've reached Mike's joint. You know what to do, so just do it."

He stopped chewing long enough to listen to the incoming message. The twerpy nasal voice was familiar to him right away. It said: "I know what to do all right. And I hope you like spending time in Mike's joint because you may soon find you don't have Mike's Porsche to take you anywhere else. And if you find this message frightening, then you're not as dumb as we think."

The big guy placed his hands before his chest and wriggled his fingers comically, a gesture he learned not from Oliver Hardy but from the merry Skipper on "Gilligan's Island." In a dainty voice he said, "Oh I'm so scared I could crap my panties."

Instead of soiling his panties, he chose to get some shoes on and grab some fast food from someplace.

***

Adam took a second look at the columns and columns of Mike and Michael Smiths hoping, irrationally, that he'd figure something out. His phone rang.

"Hello!" he cried, as if crying for help from the bottom of a cistern.

A couple miles to the west, Lori Nelson, the shapely Scandinavian with the provocative breasts and the pouty top lip, stood at the island in her kitchen, reading a brochure that promoted a leadership conference in Seattle. Into the phone, she said, "Adam? Hey, it's Lori. From Teletech. Now what's the deal?" She then chose the speakerphone option and set the phone aside in order to multitask.

"Hey, thanks for calling back! Good. Good. Listen, I mean, I really need those jeans. Can you give me that guy's number after all?"

"So you do want to talk to him?"

"Yes."

"And you're sound of mind?"

"Yes. Ha. Yes."

"Well, it wouldn't matter. He won't answer unless he knows the caller. And even then he probably won't. I bet his phone rang five times on the way to that thing last night, and each time he'd look at the caller ID and make this awful sneer. It was pretty gross. I should've leapt from the car like a hostage would."

"But we officially met last night, he and I. I shook hands with the man."

"Listen to yourself."

"Say what?"

"He doesn't know you. He doesn't know your name. I'm not sure he knows my name."

"I could leave a message."

"Sure, if he doesn't hang up before you get the chance. And if you do leave a message, he'll certainly ignore it."

"You sure know a lot about this guy, Lori."

"I'm pretty good at figuring guys out, like, really fast."

Adam looked at the nearest clock. "Awesome. Awesome. Where's he live then? I can forget the phone call and just go ahead and bust by and knock on his door."

"Look, I don't know."

"You know everything about him but you don't know where he lives?"

"We went out a total of once. Last night. He picked me up."

"Picked you up?"

"Not like that! From my place. What I mean is he came and got me. Honked from the parking lot, actually. Honked and honked in that damn pin-striped Porsche of his until the neighbors were peeping through their blinds. So I hardly know the guy and I certainly don't know where he lives."

"If I could just talk to him," he begged.

She drummed her fingers on the island. "So what's with these jeans? Why are they so special?"

"They have sentimental value."

She looked at the clock. "Well, hmm. This whole thing seems strange."

"Yeah. Strange but kind of urgent."

"So, hmm. God, let me think. You're not gonna go away easily, are you? Okay, hmm. So let's try this. Okay, what am I doing here? Jesus. Okay, maybe if you use my phone and my name is what flashes on his . . . yeah, let's try that. Your only chance is he'll recognize my name and maybe answer. So just come on over if it's so urgent."

The plan struck Adam as a little bizarre. The simple solution would be for her to give him the telephone number and be done with it. Why did she feel the need to manage the situation like that, anyway? He wondered if she wanted to see him for another reason. Obviously she wasn't dating anyone. And, hell, he was a decent-looking guy. And he had been toning up and eating more greens of late. Maybe it was that simple. But, it must be noted, she was the last woman Adam wanted anything to do with, despite those knockers and those lips and that halfway beguiling manner of hers—and . . . and anyway there wasn't the time to ponder such distractions or to conduct a character audit when millions of dollars were at stake and the lottery ticket was in peril. Only one thing mattered: Lori had the phone number he needed.

So he said "Excellent."

"I'm in the Deer Run Apartments."

"Deer Creek you mean?"

"I happen to know where I live. Deer Creek's right across the way, the one everybody gets mixed up with Deer Woods."

"That's right. It is confusing. They dammed up that really nice creek and put Deer Run there, and then later they got rid of those woods and put Deer Creek there."

"Just go to Deer Creek. I mean Deer Run. I'm in Deer Run. The signage upfront is clear. It has a sketch of a deer running. There are lots of bullet holes on the sign. The other sign, the Deer Creek sign, shows a deer drinking from a creek. There are lots of bullet holes on that sign too. I guess since all the deer got displaced, these poor guys have to shoot at something. Anyway, I'm in two-sixteen. Second building on the right."

"Got it. Two-sixteen."

"Like I said, if you call him from my phone, he'll see my name and maybe he'll answer, if he's horny. But you'll have, like, five seconds before he realizes it's not me and hangs up."

"Sounds like a winner. But are you sure I'm not troubling you? It is Saturday night."

"We can't have you going through life in your undershorts."

***

Nate Walker's typical wardrobe made no sense for his line of work: stealing cars. The lanky black man wore clothes that were stylish in the nineteen-seventies and were perhaps paroled after decades of languishing in garbage bags in the basements of thrift stores. His style, a sort of "retro shabby flashy," had originated at a Halloween party the previous fall, where it brought him so much positive attention, especially from the ladies, that he kept on dressing that way—even at his mother-in-law's wake. At least Nate's shoes made functional sense: he always wore high-top sneakers in case he ever needed to run for his life.

Even riskier, Nate had begun targeting high-end vehicles in the exclusive neighborhoods out south. He'd never felt good about stealing junkers and klunkers from the run-down apartment complexes or big-box parking lots. After all, his victims there were working folks just like he was. But the luxury cars out south . . . well, he enjoyed making life partly shitty for the very rich.

It's probably a general rule of thumb that stealing anything in broad daylight is less wise than stealing after dark, especially for a flamboyant black man in the flushest of suburbs in the heart of the heartland. But even now, as sleepy clouds drifted by the falling sun and drooped like drowsy lids, Nate just couldn't wait another minute. So he headed straight for

Sylvan Meadows in his ratty white van that squeaked and rumbled off key. The van looked like a service vehicle, which was intentional, and for additional cover he wore a hard-hat and a bright safety vest that was barely brighter than the shirt beneath it, which had slanty purple and yellow stripes, long faded but forever loud. On the floorboard lay two orange safety cones.

Soon after Nate had penetrated Sylvan Meadows, a sporty car glided towards him, driven by a big guy in expensive shades who was drinking from a straw. After it passed, Nate kept an eye on it through the rear-view mirror, and when its brake lights brightened he turned his head to confirm what the mirror suggested: the Porsche was entering a driveway. Nate swerved to the side of the road, got out, and set up the orange cones at either end of his van, and then in his costume of hardhat and safety vest he walked briskly, his head rotating in all directions like a soldier's. He reached Mike Smith's grass just as the rear fender of the Porsche disappeared inside the garage.

Nate's challenge was to get inside undetected before the garage door began to fall. He scampered the final few steps and then squatted near the edge and peeked inside. His eyes were drawn to a hand that reached for a button beside a door. Nate fell to all fours and scuttled inside a split second before the man could press that button, and he settled there, concealed by the car. A minute later, when the door was down and the man was inside his home, the lighting dimmed and died. Things got as dark as sin. With his penlight, Nate found a second interior door right where he hoped one would be, on the southeast side, which led to the side yard. He was tickled to death to see that door; it would be his only quick means of escape in case someone from the inside came out unexpectedly. Next, he skulked back to the Porsche and trained his light inside it and spotted the ignition key, which shone alone on a ring, flat on the passenger seat. Jazzed by his success so far, he was tempted to snatch the car right now. He eyed the remote-control device on the visor. *Would that white dude or whoever else in there hear the door goin' up*? he asked himself. Of course, the answer was *Yes*. He knew the safer plan would be to wait it out. A rich white guy like this probably wouldn't stay home on a Saturday night. Yet, he couldn't wait for too long because that ratty van of his was out there, unattended, screaming for attention. Hoping his chance was mere minutes away, Nate grabbed the ignition key. Next, he opened a walk-in cabinet along the east wall and stuffed himself inside it.

***

Gino's Gentlemen's Club occupied a structure that once housed a Chinese restaurant until rumors of kitchen mischief were strong enough to shutter its doors. Gino's design team retained the red door but remade the rest of the restaurant to seem less Mandarin. It was now lit in liquid yellows and blues. The building was dwarfed by an older high-rise to the east. To the west its parking lot adjoined a green space with a tiny pond, where gaggles of geese did as they pleased.

By now it was dark, and so the headlights on a cherry-red Porsche glowed as it made its way into Gino's parking lot. The driver, Mike Smith, nudged his sunglasses to the crown of his head so he could more easily find a "primo" parking spot, and right away one opened in the front row, as if obligated to. Assuredly, this man expected to be the center of attention at all times, but he had no idea he was being surveilled from at least one parked vehicle nearby, an early-nineties gray Ford Tempo. Inside it, the small figure of Fabrizio Leone punched the steering wheel. He said, "You called it, man. We only been here ten minutes and there he is. Man, I hate it when you're right."

Pleased with his prediction, Scotty squealed in laughter. "The man told us he loves the naked ladies. And it's the only nudie bar for miles."

"They actually naked in there?"

"Not just naked, Fobb. Totally naked. See the sign?"

Fabrizio made two fists and shook them as if piloting a war plane. "You know what burns my ass? Dude won't pay his debts, but he's got the balls to spring for a lap dance. And he can go ahead and stuff dollar bills between a lady's tits. Those are my dollar bills and yours too. Those should be our tits, Scotty, if life was fair."

Their two heads nearly collided above the dashboard as they leaned in to watch the loathsome figure strut to the door.

"Look at that. He's like a big dumb show-off," appraised Scotty. "Let's just take his car, Fobb. Hold it as collateral. He'll know we're serious then."

Fabrizio leaned back and scratched at his fuzzy chin. "But a car like that, you gotta think there's all kinds of security gizmos." He sighed once. He sighed a second time, but louder. "So what's our plan? Or we gonna sit here all night and just wait to follow him home?"

"Sit here all night?" Scotty shook his head. "How long you think he'll be in there? Personally, I'm not gonna lie: I'm already bored and kinda starving."

"Why would I know how long he'll be in there?"

Scotty stretched his thumb and index finger into the shape of a shark's open mouth. He turned to face his friend. "We're so close. His car is so close I can even read the license plate. Hey, wait! If you know the plate number, can you get the address from the DMV?"

"Used to you could, but then somebody raised a stink about being scared, and so now you gotta know somebody on the inside."

"Well, still, the man's so close right now," said Scotty, pointing at the structure. "Seems a shame not to do somethin'."

"I know he's in there. You know, it's startin' to drive me crazy the way you always explain the obvious to me, like I'm stupid and just don't get it."

"Whatever, man. I'm just sayin'. I mean, the truth is—"

Suddenly something happened. It was very strange.

"You see what I see?" Fabrizio asked in a whisper.

What these amateur bookies saw was a colorfully clad figure lurking at the driver's door of Mike Smith's Porsche, some forty feet away.

"What the hell's he doing?" Fabrizio asked, focusing so hard that his eyes trembled. "I don't think he's stickin' Jack Tatum on the windshield."

Astonished, they watched the man insert a key into the lock and climb inside. In the space of five seconds, the Porsche screeched backward, screeched forward, and disappeared.

"Did you see that?" Scotty asked.

Fabrizio struck the wheel again with the fleshy part of his palm. "Dude just stole the car! You saw it. We just watched a felony. The man came and got inside and stole that car, just like that. Whoosh!"

Scotty held up an index finger. "Unless the man had the key already so he could fix it or wash it. These fake rich people, they don't do anything for themselves anymore."

"No freakin' way. You saw it. How he kept looking around all guilty and then how fast he sped off. It was jacked!"

"You know what this means? Mike Smith's gonna blame it on us. After our threats and that phone call and The Assassin and everything. He's got us on tape, you know."

"Jesus, you're right. That stupid message I left. I reached out and promised him I'd take that car. I mean, this could get hairy real fast. Grand theft auto." The little guy's voice took on a tremor now. "And who knows what kinda temper he's got. I bet you he's in love with that car. Guys like that, they love things instead of people."

"Yeah, yeah. I hear yuh, man. So let's get the hell outta here."

***

In the Deer Run apartment complex, which Adam managed not to confuse with Deer Creek or even Deer Woods, Lori's tidy kitchen smelled lightly of maple syrup. Its dominant color was an eggshell blue, which brought out a similar shade in her eyes. She wore a navy skirt and a yellow tee-shirt that many moms might claim was a size too small. Adam concluded that any shirt she wore might seem a size too small. Her hair was freshly washed, partly dried, and presently unbrushed. It smelled lemony delicious.

As a guest receiving a favor, Adam put their touchy history aside, brief as it was, and smiled warmly. "Like you said, the call needs to come from your phone. Caller ID and all. It makes total sense." He backed up until his tailbone was flush against the center island. He noticed for the first time a cute dappling of freckles around her nose.

She lifted an index finger. "Hang on. You got here so quickly. I figured you'd be knocking on two-sixteen over at Deer Creek right about now. Let me grab that phone. I've got it charging down the hall."

She stepped away.

"Thanks again, man."

"Is this an elaborate ploy to get inside my pants?" she called from a hallway.

"It's my pants I'm interested in at the moment."

"Whatever," she said, returning.

While Lori tried to locate her calling history—it was a new phone and she was still all-thumbs with it—Adam used the time to gaze upon her boobs, which were no less beguiling this time around. He even felt a surge of warmth from toes to crown at the prospects of their putting aside their silly differences and working together like this. Goosebumps sprouted along his bare shins and arms. His eyes misted a little.

"You know what?" he began with a lilt. "It's awful nice of you to help me out like this. On a Saturday night no less. And if this all works out, there's gonna be a little something in it for you."

Distracted by her phone, she said, "Right. Right. Why can't I find this? These stupid phones. I keep ending up on the previous screen."

"I think you'll like it," he added in a singsong manner. "The thing that's in it for you."

"Truth is, I usually don't. A-ha, this must be his number."

"You don't like a fast hundred grand?"

"What?" she asked, finally looking at him.

"I said You don't like a fast hundred grand?"

"Do you want the number or not?"

His smile leveled and his voice got weaker with each syllable "Lori, I'm serious. I might be worth six million."

She was indeed a quick-study. Her mouth formed a bigger triangle as she came a step closer. "It's you that won the lottery?"

He too came a step closer. His arms summoned a call for caution. "I might have. Might have. But my ticket's in those damn jeans, so I can't be sure if the numbers match up."

"Wait. So you bought a ticket. Big deal."

"But I bought it at the time and the place where the winning ticket was sold, and nobody's come forward."

"But they sell hundreds an hour there."

"But the latest news said it was sold at twelve-fourteen. And that matches when I was there. I mean, I can't swear it was twelve-fourteen, but I know it was really close. And don't you think the winner would've come out by now?"

"Hang on. Hang on. You're sure about all this? That there's a real chance?"

He pointed at her floor. "Why else would I be here? On a Saturday night?"

"Jesus." Lori pursed her lips and nodded a while. "So, Adam, what I'm hearing is this: you're offering me a hundred grand."

He pointed at her. "Yes, just by giving me his number. Because you'll be helping me get the ticket back without tipping off that Mike Smith guy. He cannot be told why I want those jeans."

He managed to smile at the smile she'd so quickly formed. Despite the executive suits, the buzzwords, and the naked ambition, she really was decent people.

She said, "A measly hundred grand is what you're telling me?"

"What?"

She waved the phone. "Without this number, you will never see those jeans again."

"Are you serious?"

Her eyes were narrow, her teeth cocked. He could see her jaw muscles pulsing just below the temple.

"Oh come on. For God's sake."

She formed a fist around the phone and pulled it tight to her gut.

"Okay, be that way. A million, Lori. You get a million. I don't care. What do I care? I could never spend six million. Besides, the love of money is the root of all evil."

As she folded her arms, the tiny phone disappeared within her bosom. "Half."

"Half a million? Okay. Okay. Jesus. So you are a little reasonable after all."

"Half of six million," she clarified, grinning with just her teeth.

He stood slack-mouthed for two seconds, and then: "Get lost! Get lost, Lori. Just go ahead and get lost!"

"Oh you want me to get lost, huh? But I'm the one in control here. I have the phone number and I know about the ticket. And the minutes are ticking away. He'll find that thing soon enough if he hasn't already."

"Jesus, you're cold-blooded."

"If I were so cold-blooded, would I be giving you half?"

"I think I might hate you. Because you know what you sound like? You sound like a greedy, ambitious man. We don't need any more of those."

"Half," she said.

He spat a laugh and threw his arms all over the place. "Lady, I swear. What can I do? You've got me cornered. You know what? You've now cost me three-million bucks. Ha, I better get a good-night kiss out of this."

She raised a yellow brow. "That will cost you more."

By now they were near enough to effect such a kiss; the heated exchange had drawn them closer, line by line, step by step. And passions were hotly lit, of course. For three long seconds they engaged in a staring contest, until Lori glanced at the purple device that shivered in her palm. She peeped a squeak, stepped back, and said, "God oh God, three million." Gripping her gut, she charged around a corner and slammed the bathroom door behind her.

Adam grabbed his own gut. "You got another john?"

"Way down the hall! You'll find it!"

Rushing in that direction, he said, "Rich people must take a lotta craps."

***

A few miles from Lori's bathrooms at the Deer Run apartments, Nate Walker, the flashy car thief, sat squeezed in the Porsche he'd lifted, now parked in a stall at a Sonic drive-in. He was violating one of his oldest rules, which said to take a hot car directly to the shop. But everything had gone so well so far, and he wanted to celebrate with an icy Sprite. If pressed, he'd also admit it was a trip to be inside such a car. Yes, he was tempting arrest, but maybe he was safer in that car than anyone might think. In that part of town, the cops might presume a black man in a shiny Porsche was a millionaire receiver on the Kansas City Chiefs or, more likely, a drug dealer who'd bought the car fair and square with his own bundles of cash.

The soda cup tottered between his thighs as he stretched to scour the glove box. He found nothing valuable there, just a scattering of fast-food napkins, some Toby Keith and Phil Collins CDs, and a flattened St. Louis Cardinals baseball cap. When he finally backed from the stall, a rear tire rolled over a head of lettuce and the disturbance sent the Sprite sloshing all over his crotch.

"Damn lids never fit right!"

Upon leaning to get the napkins from the glove box, he noticed Adam's wadded jeans darkening the dark floorboard. It was a happy discovery, for his balls were drenched.

***

In the kitchen of unit two-sixteen, Adam Durham orbited Lori Nelson's island at a speed that suggested he was racing, not pacing. There was a lot on his mind, he couldn't focus, and he was struggling to get used to a couple big ideas: that he might be worth three million dollars and that he might've been worth six million if this woman wasn't a vulture.

Forcing such distractions aside, he said, "A guy like that, I'm sure he's gone through the pockets by now."

"But you said he saw you take out your wallet and keys."

"I think he did. But still. I mean, there are some things in life we just have to do. A kid can't pass a drinking fountain without taking a slurp, right? A billboard? You have to read it, even when you don't want to. And if a friend hands you a book and says it's really good, what do you do?"

"You want me to answer that?"

"Yes."

"Well, you open it somewhere in the middle. You glance at that page. And then you fan through the rest of the pages for five seconds as if that proves something."

"Exactly! And it's the same with pockets. Everyone goes through pockets. A neighbor kid picked up thrift store donations, and he spent half his days rifling through pockets. But, heck, at least that ticket's just a little slip of paper in a back pocket. You could miss it pretty easy unless you plunge your hand inside and really burrow around."

"Burrow around? How big is this back pocket?"

"Or if we're lucky, maybe he's just a slob and he leaves that gym bag in the car for a long time until it stinks to high heaven."

"I don't know," she said. "He seems like a control freak. Law and order and all of that. Kind of like a serial killer, you know. Those guys always make sure everything's in its place."

"So this is all pointless then? He's seen the jeans and ransacked the pockets?"

"Probably. I mean, almost certainly. But with millions at stake, we can't presume anything." She placed her elbows on the island and jutted her shapely little butt westward in order to force her guest to widen his path and therefore slow his pace. "Okay, so back to the plan. Did we agree the plan is this? I call and sweet talk him, and he invites me over, expecting some thrills. And—"

"You sure he'll invite you over?"

"Listen to yourself, Adam. Anyway, so, where was I? Let's see: I call, he invites me over, and it's my job to somehow get my hands on your pants."

"Yes."

"Just as long as I don't have to touch his pants."

"Let's just do it." He pounded a fist into the opposite palm. "Come on. No more talking. We can't overthink this. We can't look for . . . benchmarks and metrics and all that. Every minute's precious."

"That's easy for you to say because I'll be the one doing the ugly work." She moved closer and jabbed an index finger in the direction of his gut. "I mean, you'll be on your couch spooning chili from a can while I'm trapped in his house, scheming to get to those damn jeans of yours. They could be anywhere, Adam. In his car. In the garbage. I don't know. And this Mike Smith isn't the type of guy who wants some chick to go digging around his corners and closets."

"Fine. Then let's make a better plan, but let's do it fast. We have to go fast."

Lori opened a kitchen drawer and got out a pen and a yellow pad.

Adam hated the sight of yellow pads. "How complicated will this get?"

She placed the pad on the island. "Nothing wrong with getting our strategy on paper."

"Strategy?"

"You know. Like, a brain dump."

"Are you kidding me?"

She backed away from the island and the pad. With her hands on either side of her head, she said, "Just shut up and grow up and let's figure this out. You're being so high-maintenance, Adam!"

"All right, all right. Whatever."

"All right?"

"Yes. Continue."

With that out of the way, she said, "Okay, where were we? Yes. Now the big question is Once I'm inside, how do I break away to find your jeans without raising suspicion? That's what we have to figure out for now."

They both looked downward while they thought things through. Lori tapped a fist to her lips and Adam scratched at the back of his neck with both hands. After ten seconds, he spoke first.

"We could try this: Let's presume the gym bag's still in the car, okay? And so maybe you suggest a pizza run. Then when his car's stopped at a light, you grab the bag and run like mad."

"Sweet. Very sweet, except for two things that come immediately to mind. One, despite our best wishes, the bag probably isn't in the car. And, two, this isn't Wally Cleaver we're talking about. This guy isn't even Eddie Haskell. He's not gonna want to go out for pizza. He'll just want to hit the love sack once I'm there. I mean, what else is there to do? It's been established that we hate each other."

"Okay. Probably so. Bedroom then. Bedroom. Hmm." After three seconds, he snapped his fingers. "Maybe you could tie him to the bed and then go seize the bag, wherever it is."

"Tie the man up?"

"Sometimes things go in that direction, don't they? I mean, that's what I've heard."

"Oh. It's gonna go in that direction, this plan of ours?"

Adam shrugged. "Are you into bondage, Lori?"

"Actually, I was hoping to be in his place for, like, nineteen seconds." She clapped twice. "Hey, maybe this! What if I don't mess around at all? I mean, what if I charge inside and tell him I'm so mad at you because you made a crude pass at me last night?"

"No, It's gotta be realistic. He's not that dumb."

"Hear me out!" She clasped her hands at her chin and pushed them outward to stress key syllables. "Speaking hypothetically and all, maybe I tell him how much I hate and detest you. That you're just a typical jerk who tries to look sensitive and smart by brooding around and stuff. Yes! And . . . and I say you're one of those guys who makes fun of rich guys and calls 'em phony sell-outs all the time just because you feel inadequate. Yes. And I tell him I want your pants so I can cut 'em to shreds. Because you make my flesh creep and my skin crawl!"

A chill tickled the top of his spine. "It might work. It actually might."

"It might! But if it fails, the game's over."

"Over?"

"Because he's gonna know for sure that your pants are somewhere in his possession, and he'd go straight to the pockets."

"What other choice do we have by now?" he asked. "He's either seen 'em or he hasn't. I don't know. I'm feeling jumpy about all this. Let's just do something and see what happens."

"Something?"

"Just call him and let's see how it goes."

"Are you always this impatient?"

"Yes. But . . . hell, you're clever, right? We probably are overthinking this. Call him up."

"You're sure about that?"

"I can't take it any longer," he grieved. "These schemes all sound desperate and doomed. Maybe it'll be a relief to get bad news at this point."

"All right. Whatever. It's your funeral." She reached for the little rectangular device and then looked him square in the eyes.

"You mean, you're actually gonna call him now?"

"Adam, for once you're probably right. Yes, I can think on my feet. Okay? And like you said, it probably is best to do something. Time is short."

And so the young woman spent the next few minutes phoning and re-phoning her blunt-faced date from the night before. After the fourth try, she put the phone on the yellow pad on the island. "He's simply not answering. Not a surprise, really."

"You made a nice impression on him last night."

"He's a bastard. I'm honored he hates me."

Adam resumed pacing around the island, slower laps this time. "So where'd you meet him?"

"At a happy hour, okay," she snapped, more angry at herself than at him.

"I bet that was a barrel of monkeys."

"Stay on task. And please stop with the pacing. It's so dizzying. I feel like one of those blonde chicks in a Hitchcock movie."

"So who was he with anyway? Maybe that can shed some light."

"He came on to me from out of nowhere. I think he was alone. Some guys do that, you know. Go to bars alone and prey on women."

"And he preyed on you? That kind of surprises me, actually."

"What are you implying?"

"No, it's . . . a compliment, sort of."

"I wouldn't say 'preyed' on me. These things are complicated. They're situational and all. Lots of, like, nuances. And too much alcohol."

"Wait. Nuance and alcohol? Those don't seem to go together."

"You've never been a woman."

"It's all good, Lori." He backed against the kitchen table. "But can't you recall any clues to where he might live?"

"I'm trying. I've been trying. He really had nothing to say. I mean, he talked about himself a lot, but I stopped listening. I do know he likes that one country-boy comedian. The 'git-er-done' guy. He said 'git-er-done' two or three times on the ride over last night. It's a miracle I didn't kill him."

"Man, we've gotta figure this out, Lori. I need that money so I never have to go inside Teletech Penitentiary ever again and sit through another lame-ass meeting."

She shrugged.

"Oh, now don't tell me you'd keep working."

"What's it to you?" she said.

"Nothing. Nothing at all." This was finally too much. If he had a cigarette, he'd have smoked it. If he had a beer, he'd have chased it with whiskey.

"No, you can elaborate," she said.

"I'm just saying that some people actually like the workplace."

"Wow. They should be shot."

"Wait. That's not where I'm going with this. No, I was gonna say I suppose they're lucky in that regard. I'm even jealous in a way. Back in college, my dorm roommate was this guy from Joplin, an accounting major, and he fell asleep every night the moment he shut his eyes, and he never woke up in the middle of the night for any reason, not even to pee."

"So what?"

He halted and turned. "So, life is simple for some people. And life is simpler for people who like to go to the office. That's all I'm saying."

"Some people make life harder than it needs to be," she retorted.

He made a fist and shook it at nothing. "That damn Monique. If she hadn't shown up in that bikini, I'd have never changed out of those jeans and I'd be a millionaire right now and you wouldn't."

Amused, she said, "Ah, so you like Monique? So you're attracted to ditzy women?"

He shook his head.

"Submissive women then? Women who pose no threat?"

"That's not what—"

"Adam Durham, are you intimidated by women who are smarter than you?"

"Soon as I meet one, I'll be sure to let you know."

Lori's mouth gaped and her hands went straight to her hips. "Oh boy. Oh ho. I am now speechless. You have rendered me speechless, young man."

He was grinning too hard to reply.

She smiled too. It brought out her dimples and something different in her eyes. "Ha. Pretty proud of yourself? You think you're clever?"

"I have my moments."

"So that's what makes you happy. Wisecracks."

"You're into wisecracks yourself, Lori. I'm just trying to keep up."

"Why do you hate your job so much? You believe you're too good to do whatever it is you do in that strange little corner on the second floor there? You believe you should be writing screenplays or books or rock-and-roll ballads or what?"

"Yes. Books, probably."

His honesty surprised her. "Well, then that . . . that would explain some things. Ah-ha, I bet you were an English major."

He leaned against the kitchen table again. "What's wrong with that?"

"Not a thing."

"Books were my best friends when I was young. Plus they helped me sit still. The good ones did."

Now her grin was purely victorious. "I'm just saying I've seen your type before. You're all sad and sensitive and full of it. You're mad at yourself for not being a big-shot writer or poet or whatever, and that frustration touches everything in your life. Right? I've got you all figured out."

"Man, we've known each other for nine minutes and you've got me all figured out. Why do you even care what I'm all about?"

She held out a palm as if stopping traffic. "No, you're right. You're right. That all came out harsher than I wanted. It's just that I'm sure you've been making some big assumptions about me, and so . . . ."

"Tell you what: How about we pledge to keep this thing impersonal from now on? We've already wasted precious minutes on all this nonsense. Trying to outwit each other or whatever. The thing is, I don't care what makes you tick and you don't care what makes me tick. And once we each have three million in our separate little fists, we can move to our separate tropical islands and never see each other again."

"Promise?"

"So, about those jeans?" he replied.

For the next few minutes they wracked their minds and muttered feeble fragments and ineffectual oaths while circling that square island. Until Adam stopped so abruptly that Lori bumped into him and had to clutch his waist for balance. He snapped his fingers. She backed away. He turned.

"I might have an idea."

"I'm all ears," she said.

"Okay. Good. Are you listening?"

"I just said I'm all ears."

"Okay then. It's a longshot, but we have to try something."

***

Not far from Sonic, the hot Porsche idled by a dumpster behind a big box store that had gone belly-up long before. In the darkness, Nate Walker stood in his shirt, socks, and skivvies. He hoped the open passenger door would help shield his family parts, just in case, but he was too tall for that. Though no other creatures were stirring nearby, not even rodents, the look on his face said a vehicle could heave into view at any moment and complicate things. And the cops out that way were thick. Nate knew he needed to hurry. He looked both ways and then tossed his checkered, soda-soaked slacks onto the passenger seat. Before putting on the dry jeans, he took the briefest of moments to "bunny ear" the front pockets and to pat down the back ones, which felt empty to the touch. Just as distant headlights swept across his face, he pressed one leg into the jeans and then, awkwardly, the second leg. It was a tight fit already. He forced the jeans upward and upward, twisting them and his leg in opposite directions while hopping flat-footedly.

***

In southern Johnson County, the old, gray Tempo snailed between stoplights with hundreds of other vehicles on a six-lane boulevard, a road that looked like dozens of others nearby. Nobody inside those other autos could've been half as frustrated as Fabrizio and Scotty. The driver's tiny hands were white on the wheel.

"Man, I feel so helpless," he said. "I hate that feeling."

"Maybe we go back to the strip club and wait him out like we first planned."

"That was a big-ass felony we saw there, Scotty. A car got ripped right before our eyes. It's best we keep away from it, right?"

"But at least we'll know where he is. We can keep an eye on him while we figure something out. He'll be inside a while, and we can use that time to think. And then we just follow him home like we planned all along."

"You were the bored one, remember? The starving one? But okay. We should go back to the first plan. Put a tail on him. See if we can't find out where he lives. But wait. How the hell's he gettin' home? A taxi or what?"

"That's right. He's got no car no longer. This is so tricky."

"Anyways, we can't bother with that side of it. He'll need to get home; it ain't my problem. I'm not some kinda' travel agent. And like I said all along, once we get his home address, it gives me time to figure things out.

He'll become, like, a sitting duck. We'll figure out a way to get what's ours."

"Knowledge is power, Fobb. Knowledge is power."

***

In his bungalow near the northern end of the county, Nate stood by the TV, sipping from what remained of his Sprite and altogether grinning while his pudgy wife eyed him suspiciously, her hands on her hips, her head swayed back like a cobra's. The only thing that ever brought joy to this marriage was their bickering—and by all accounts this was a happy marriage.

"What you been up to?" Florina's head got stationary but her eyes darted upward and downward and upward again. Finally they settled on his bare shins.

"Picked a good one out there tonight. Oh baby it's sweet!"

"Why's it in this here driveway and not in the damn shop? Huh? You hate me so much you wanna go to prison and be off by yourself inside them four gates?"

"I wanted to show you for real that I ain't a sack a' shit like you're always sayin'. Look at that thing out there, doll."

"I seen it through the curtains already!"

"First off, I scoped it out. Then second off, I played it smart. I made sure I got the key in my own hands, you see. And then I waited inside his cubby hole for the white cat to get his extra key and then go drive it someplace. And then I ran outside and got into the van and followed it and he never once caught on. And when he got out and went inside this one place, I snatched the wheels for my own."

"Slow down, fool. You can't tell a good story for shit. How'm I posta to follow all them twists and turns like that?"

"Baby, all that matters is merchandise like that go for sixty large at least."

"Cubby hole? What kinda man is this?"

"I bet you never thought your ol' man could bring home a ride like that. I'll be famous when I take it in. They'll name a statue after me."

She circled him, hands on hips, and made lots of sound effects, long familiar to him, that implied suspicion and scorn. "What about them pants? You steal the man's pants as well? You don't own no pants like that. And they sure as hell don't fit your sorry ass. Or maybe you been out with some trampy whore?"

He snickered. "That's right. A trampy whore gimme these jeans."

She raised to her toes and positioned her face nearer to his. "Where you get 'em at?"

"They were just sittin' in that car I stole. What happened was I spilt my pop on my own pants, so I had to put these on."

"For real?"

"Girl, my own pants was soppin' wet. They're out in that car right now. Forgot to bring 'em inside. That's another reason I come home in the first place. To change into some dry pants of my own."

Florina charged for the door. "Your pants best be in that car and they best smell like your ass!"

Unfazed by the threats, he took a final drink as the front door spanked its frame. Quickly she returned, his checkered pants bunched in her arms. In stride, she heaved them at him, Rick Barry style. "Get outta them things and inside a hot bath! You don't know where them pants been! I'm gonna start the washin' machine!"

"Why you throw 'em at me then if you headin' for the washin' machine?"

Looking behind her without slowing, she said, "Because it's all I had in my hands!"

"Ain't got the time for a hot bath," Nate mumbled as she vanished around the corner. "I gotta get that car to the shop and collect my capital gains."

He dropped his wadded, wetted pants on the living-room floor before turning a different corner, opening a dresser, and pulling out a separate pair of checkered slacks. Before he could unlace his shoes, his beeper beeped. He sat on the edge of his bed and looked at it. "Damn emergency code," he said aloud. He looked in the doorway and realized she'd be back in no time, with additional questions, complaints, criticisms, and orders. He decided to change clothes later. He grabbed the dry slacks and raced from the room.

***

In her lightly colored, lightly lit bedroom, Lori Nelson sat erect in a swivel chair at her computer station, her bare feet flat on the carpet. Adam Durham was beside her, a bare knee on the carpet, an elbow on the desktop. Google's search page filled the screen. She typed "mike smith" into the Advanced Search field. The result was 1,270,000 hits.

"You take the first half million, and I'll look up the rest," Adam said.

"It was your stupid idea." She clicked the Back button and added asshole to the description. The resulting screen showed 120,528 hits.

"Please don't do an image search on that one," he said.

"Wait! That's an idea."

"Oh God no."

She deleted asshole and then chose the option for an image search, but the results were mostly a gallery of mug shots of men who were not the Mike Smith they needed, though many of them looked just as offensive and seemed to be posing for the police or a fraternity brother. She scrolled and scrolled before rolling her chair away from the desk and slumping in it.

"Can't we put in more adjectives?" Adam asked. "Because I've got plenty."

"Dumb idea."

"What about his phone number? Let's search it and see if it hooks us up to an address."

"I did that first, when you were off peeing the first time, because I knew that searching by such a common name like Mike Smith would be a waste of time. But I got zilch. It's hard to track down a mobile number and get it matched up to an address. I've tried it before. Now, a landline, you have a fighting chance of getting the address for that."

"God, yes, his landline. If only we had that number, we could match it up to his address in the phone book."

"It's unlisted. I did learn that much last night. He said he used to get way too many calls from the dorks in India, as he put it, and so he went unlisted a couple years ago."

"Groovy. More good news for us." He pushed away from the desk and skulked until his back was against her bed frame.

She sat up even straighter and pointed at the newspaper that was spread open on her bed, just beyond his shoulder. "Go look at those winning numbers again. Do they look familiar?"

"I told you, I just don't know. I barely looked at the ticket when I bought it."

"Did you even bother to sign it?"

"I had a banana in my hand."

"You should've signed it, I think."

"Well, maybe you're right. I don't know."

"So, you don't have a system for choosing the numbers?"

"This was the first time I've ever bought one. Hell, for all I know, the guy coulda given me a ticket to the police circus. That's how close I looked."

"God, what even drove you to buy a lottery ticket in the first place?"

"It's a long story."

Lori rolled up to him in her executive chair, which took some effort on that thick carpet. Then she leaned forward and purred, "Maybe if you get into a deep state of relaxation you'll recall the numbers."

"Relax at a time like this?"

"You ever been hypnotized?"

"Just once. By a very nice set of knockers."

"Ha. Well, if that's what it takes."

Adam blushed. He looked away.

She backed off again. "But no, you can tell I'm really grasping here. Just trying to do anything so I won't have to call that crumb again."

After a moment, he said, "Would it make any sense to pore through every Mike Smith in the white pages and highlight those addresses that at least seem feasible? Yeah, and then we can triage the locations and drive by each one and see if we spot his car?"

"Focus, please! I just told you he's unlisted. Ergo, he's not in the phone book. You do have a problem focusing sometimes, don't you?"

He got to his feet and started pacing as best he could in that tiny bedroom.

She said, "I guess I have to call him again. Who knows? Maybe I'll wear him down and he'll answer one of these times. I guess I have no other choice."

"This time go ahead and leave a message. What do you think?"

"Arrghh. It's probably time to do just that."

"I suppose we should go the flirtatious route after all and not let him know about the jeans. Make him think you're all . . . horny or something."

She nodded. "The other way—trashing you—would be more fun, but, yeah. We're stuck between a rock and a hard place."

"Cool. So please just leave a sexy message or whatever."

***

Inside the gentlemen's club, Mike Smith felt at peace. It was not a foreign sensation, for the man was totally secure in his beliefs and ethics and had no particular demons to deal with and certainly nothing to apologize for. But tonight he deserved a special treat after what he'd been put through the evening before, when that stuck-up broad tried to give him a hard time in front of other people. And now, the nerve of it—she was calling him over and over, no doubt to beg forgiveness and beg for a second chance. Well, Mike Smith despised her, but he was smart enough to keep his options open. If nothing better came along, he might call the broad later and then proceed to poke her all night long, no questions asked. It wouldn't break his heart to get a long look at those tits of hers. Yes, Gino's was a nice spot for a fellow like Mike Smith to unwind. There were lots of classy guys in there, some of them in neckties, and they almost outnumbered the greasy slime balls who couldn't afford such pleasures in the first place. So, amid the comforts of the pulsating dance beat, the racing strobe lights, and the hooting, shouting, and catcalls, Mike Smith settled in for a lap dance, which put a blissful grin on his face, unbroken by the two manufactured breasts that stabbed at his cheeks. Any patrons who happened to study his facial expression—which would have been a shame, considering the alternative viewing options—might've found it heartening, for it was as pure as the smiles that adults put on when they see a child in a tuxedo or watch Pete Seeger in song.

But all good things must end, even in Mike Smith's world. Soon his nirvana got violated by a vibration from within his pants. He reached and tilted his head just enough to see the name Lori Nelson on the caller ID. "I knew it," he whispered. He flicked the phone shut and said to the dancer "Somebody really likes Mike."

***

Nate Walker and the Porsche 911 were finally side by side and safe in the shop, which except for its tinted windows looked like a mechanic's garage. All six bays were filled with stolen autos, mostly domestic SUVs. The crew chief, Harvey, was paunchy and grizzled, his hair the color of gunpowder, his grayish face poisoned by fifty years of cigarettes, fumes, and vending machine fare. His young assistant, Willy, sported the kind of jumbo afro rarely seen beyond the decade of the seventies, one so large that strangers might be forgiven if they thought he was in costume for a skit. In fact, Willy's afro would've been more fitting on Nate's head, owing first to the thief's retro attire and, second, to his adult age since it seemed that Willy couldn't have lived long enough to have grown such a sizable thing on his head. Together, the old guy and the kid sized up the Porsche while Nate stood behind them, surprised they were not leaping for joy.

"Why'd you beep me like that? I don't see no emergency."

"Because you're an early bird, Nate. I was expecting to hear from you earlier. Wanted to make sure you didn't get pinched. We look out for each other around here, you know." Harvey stepped back and said, "And it turns out I saved you the last damn bay for this? I shoulda known you'd come in with somethin' all shiny and wild."

"This car don't kick your ass?"

"Hey, it's a fine machine. Good engineering. Savvy paint job. Some German precision for sure. But you know how the boss hates these fancy foreign trinkets. They're a big risk."

"Nobody told me that."

"I told you so last weekend," boomed Harvey. "When you brought in whatever the hell it was. Damn thing coulda made a queen blush."

Nate edged past them and the afro. "I'll just take it back then. You shoot me the damn emergency code and I rush my ass over here for what? I'm gonna take it back."

"Wait!" Harvey blocked his progress and backed against the sporty car. He folded his arms as if to signify a bulwark. "It may not be a total loss. Maybe we can figure something out. Part it out even. Maybe foist it on the Polacks."

"Part out a Porsche? Have you lost your mind and shit?"

Willy, circling Nate, said, "What the deal with yo' pants?"

"What about my pants?"

"They some for-real flood pants. And it look like yo' balls be barkin' in them things."

Harvey laughed, though he knew he shouldn't. Nate had a reputation for being sensitive. It was strange. The man happily took it when his porky wife gave him hell, which was all the time, but he could not accept needling from anyone else. Young Willy had once diagnosed the whole thing as a "mamma complex."

"Why's everyone treat me like shit around here?" Nate growled.

"Them pants makin' you walk like you forgot to wipe y'own ass."

Nate thrust a finger into the teen's shoulder. "Cat, how old are you?"

Harvey pushed a lumpy arm between their chests. "Nate! Back off. Come on. We got work to do, guys. We got good people out there expectin' a quality service. Willy, get back to the Windstar. Nate, you go ahead and sit down up there on that barstool up by the candy-corn machine while I make a call or two. Stick around and go ahead and calm down for me, will ya? We're all on the same side here. I'll talk to you in a few minutes."

***

Meanwhile, Adam was flat on Lori's twin bed, his feet hanging off the edge and wiggling fast and nonstop, perhaps to show how much he wanted to speed things along. More than once she'd chided him for all the fidgeting. More than once he'd told her she sounded like all his teachers over the years, as well as parents, neighbors, workplace colleagues, outspoken toddlers, and total strangers.

Now Lori held her phone to her bosom as she spun in the chair to face him.

He said, "Once again you chickened out and hung up. You're supposed to leave a sexy message."

"You honestly expect me to get sexy in my bedroom? While you're in here?"

"So, should I step away for a minute?"

Exasperated, she closed her eyes and nodded. She then rose and pointed at the doorway in case there was any confusion.

"But hurry," he reminded her as he passed.

"Shut the door behind you, please."

In the hallway, he backed against the door, which had not completely closed. About an inch of daylight survived between it and the jamb. He now managed to hold still and focus on her words, and what he heard was a jolt. Lori was affecting a southern accent! And a rotten one at that! But he couldn't deny there was something very cute about its hopelessness. This strange accent had begun as a defense mechanism, but as she started to realize how foolish she sounded, she chose to double-down on it, as if to prove that all along she'd only been camping it up, that none of this was real. In any event, here are the words she left on the man's machine: "Hey, Mike. This here's Lori-Lori. Nelson. So sorry about last night. I'd really like to kiss all y'all's privates. All night long. So call me right away, y'all. Uh . . . okay then."

In a sweat, she clapped shut the phone, clapped shut her eyes, and whispered, "My God, what have I become?"

Adam re-entered, laughing. "My 'Hee-Haw honey!'"

"You dumb-ass!" She slapped after him.

But he scampered out of reach, knees high, and when he saw that Lori wasn't laughing at his physical comedy, he stopped.

"Sorry. I couldn't help it. The walls are thin here."

Soberly, she said, "Look, this isn't my thing. I'm a project manager, for God's sake." She stepped farther away and then turned sideways and looked out her window.

He took a heavy step toward her and searched for something to say.

"This is getting tough, Adam, this charade of ours. I mean, it's only been twenty minutes, but still."

After an uneasy few seconds, he said, "What if I just went ahead and called his number from my phone? That way, you get to stay out of it. You don't have to pretend to like him. I mean, you'd still get your share, of course. And so maybe he won't answer. He probably won't. But there's nothing to lose by trying."

She tapped at her pursed lips while thinking it through. "Well, I guess I could give you his number and you could put it into your phone. But you know what that would mean?" She threw her arms wide. "Suddenly I'm superfluous!"

He actually flinched. "Lori? Seriously? After all of this?"

She lifted her brows. "All of this? You mean a half-hour of amateur scheming?"

"I just said you'd keep your share."

"So I can trust you with the number? That's what you're saying? I can trust you to keep that promise? Heck, I hardly even know you, Adam."

"I thought you had me all figured out."

She bent and pointed. "See. Ah-ha! You're clever. I have to be cautious around guys like you."

"Come on, you're just messing with me now. Look, you can give me the number or not. Actually, screw the number. But do not think for a minute that I'm a cheat. I do not rip people off. I've got my flaws but that's not me. I have a hard enough time sleeping well when I do the right things in life. I mean, I'm not like the guy from Joplin who could fall asleep in seconds, my dorm-mate back in—"

"All right, all right. I was messing with you. So call him. Call him up. But I'll tell you what we have to lose, both of us, if you do call him. Can you focus and listen carefully while I explain?"

He backed away, groaning.

She continued: "We've agreed our best hope—maybe our only hope—is what?"

"Uh . . . that he hasn't found the jeans yet?"

"Correct. We hope they're still buried in that smelly bag of his, wherever it might be. So if I'm the one who talks with him, then this plan of ours might still work—me being flirty and all. Because that way I can get next to him without mentioning the jeans. I'll seem to have other ulterior motives, you know? In other words, my tits do the talking so your jeans can do the walking."

"I get it, I get it."

"You should get it because it's basically our original plan. Because if you call, what kind of motive could you have, huh? You want to be pals? You want a joyride in that Porsche? You'd like to play a round of miniature golf? I mean, presuming he even answers the damn call? No, you'd have to tip him off to the jeans because there's no other reason to call."

"All right," he said. "So essentially we stick to the original plan. Then, sure, let's just have your boobs do the heavy lifting."

***

Perched like a gargoyle upon a cathedral, Nate tried his best not to blow his stack. Luckily, he found a distraction an arm's length away in the form of a People Weekly. It was a few years old, but he opened it somewhere in the middle and tried to make the best of it.

Soon Harvey returned, a fresh smoke waggling in his grayish lips. "Boss said we can give you twenty percent of your normal take."

Nate was so staggered, he could hardly muster a voice. "That's an insult, Harvey."

Leaning in, the old guy said, "Come again?"

Nate repeated his remark more loudly, as shock turned to outrage.

Shrugging, the old guy said, "Comes down to risk versus reward."

"That a lotta shit," the thief said.

Harvey took out the cigarette and held it to his thigh. "What can I say? He's got a hard-on for the domestics, for the sport-utes. Stuff that blends in and moves easy. And you bring in something like that. To move a property like that, it takes a lotta extra steps, a lotta extra risk."

"Any dawg can jack a Bronco."

"Are you even listening? This is not a competition we're running here, not some beauty pageant."

Nate dropped to his feet and got up close to the older man. "You listen to me, fool. I'm a cat that grew up in the projects and survived all kinds a wild street shit, and then a while ago I was out drivin' that sweet sweet mother-fucker right over there." He pointed at the Porsche to make sure there was no confusion. "There are cats who went to college ain't never drove a ride like that. I'm a man who's come a long way in life and now I'm stickin' it to folks who never saw nothin' in me. You feel me?"

"You didn't earn that car, Nate. You stole it."

He stamped a foot. "I bet that ride cost sixty large on the showroom floor."

Harvey advanced until the toes of his drab work shoes nearly stepped on the toes of Nate's high-tops. "Man, how many times I gotta say it? In this business you have to stay under the radar. You with all them showy clothes and flashy cars. I mean, the paisley alone gives us the cold sweats."

Nate leaned in and squinted to show Harvey he was serious. "Maybe I'll go back to work at the Wal Marts. At least they 'preciated me there."

"No they didn't."

"Least they didn't make fun of me there."

"Who can say?"

"This a lotta shit, Harvey. You know it is, man. You just know it is."

The man waved his hands and shook his head at the same time. "Listen. I don't got time to fight this battle. Take my advice as a friend. We been through a lot together. So just take the twenty percent and go ahead and forget about it. It's cash in your pocket. You're a crook, remember? You don't have time for principles. Now where's your van parked? I'll get Riley to drive you back to your van and then you can go ahead and spend your loot on whores or booze or the horses or whatever the hell you want to."

"The horses?"

"Riley!" Harvey shouted.

From the far end came the sound of a slamming door, and through it came Riley, a bow-legged black man with tufts of silver poking above the ears. He took a sidelong look at Nate and said, "Your ol' lady been dryin' your britches in the microwave?"

"Not you now."

"You expectin' the Grand Coulee Dam to bust or what?"

"This a lotta shit! I'm takin' my car away from here!" Arms swinging, Nate bypassed Riley and kept on going.

Harvey tramped after the lanky thief. "That car's been hot a while, Nate. I'm sure it's been reported by now. And look at it. You won't get past the laundromat before some cop's got you in his crosshairs." Then he turned and glared at Riley and Willy, both of whom were having a hell of a good time tittering beside the pop machine.

At the Porsche, Nate opened the driver's door, stepped out of his high-tops, tugged down Adam's jeans with all the requisite twisting and cussing, and threw them hard toward the back seat; they ended up on the floorboard there. He reached for the pair of checkered pants he'd brought along and wriggled into them, a much easier task.

Willy shook his head and elbowed Riley. "Dude's quick puttin' on them other pants leastways."

Nodding, Riley said, "Gotta give the man props for that."

***

Adam and Lori were again at her computer because they sensed the answer to Mike Smith's location lay somewhere in the guts of that thing, but the internet connection just barely crawled and the tower sounded asthmatic. Pissed by it all, Lori rose first and made for the kitchen.

"Think," said Adam from two steps behind her. "Relive last night. Every moment of it."

"I'm not eager to relive last night. And we tried this ten minutes ago and ten minutes before that."

He boosted himself onto the island as she opened the refrigerator. "Okay," he said, pointing with both index fingers, "the dude picked you up. He honked and honked out there until the neighbors were ready to call the cops. So . . . hey! What if I went outside and honked and honked? Maybe something in your memory might click."

"Right."

"It worked with Pavlov and that dog."

With her head deep into the freezer, she said, "But wait a minute." She backed away and gave an understated clap as the door grooved shut. "You might be on to something with the honking. Some of these neighbors just had to be drawn to their windows, don't you think? Maybe they saw something? Because think about it: When you hear a guy honking like that, don't you go take a really good look at him, just to see what kind of jackass is doing that?"

"But what could they have seen that might help us?"

She shrugged. "I don't know. A revealing bumper sticker?"

"Plus, to go from door to door right now, there's an opportunity cost to think about. You know what that term means?"

"You mean we could use our time doing something better," she answered. "Hey, I'm all for doing something better. Just tell me what it is. Until then, we can at least think about going door to door."

"I suppose we could do it," he said without much spirit, "but let me ask you this: You ever hear of the Immaculate Reception?"

"That football thing? The crazy catch way back in the seventies."

He got down and to his feet again. "Yes. Very good. Well, one time when I was young this radio guy, this sports-talk host, posed the question to his callers: What were you doing when you saw that miraculous catch? And as you might guess, all the callers said the same thing: I was watching the game."

"So what's your point? That all these people will tell us the same useless thing?"

"More or less," he answered.

"I'd say not necessarily, because our question would be different. It would be 'What did you see?' And everybody sees different things when they look at the same thing. Like . . . for example, Holly the intern might look at you and see a cute guy. Someone else might look at you and see a total poseur. I'm just being theoretical is all. To make a point, that is. Abstractly speaking, of course."

"I still think it's a rotten idea."

"Well . . . I'll concede this one. For once you're probably right." She then started pacing around the island in Adam's old tracks, as if he'd earlier dug ruts into the linoleum. She clasped her hands behind her back and hung her head. "Oh the love of money. It's the root of all . . . anguish."

"I'll say."

Wearing a pouty expression, she shuffled up behind him and then, as if helpless, dropped her forehead upon the back of his shoulder, where it remained just long enough for him to savor one full whiff of her lemony shampoo.

***

Months ago, the worthies who manage Thirsty Mack's held a daylong meeting with a creative firm in that firm's Special War Room, and by the close of day those minds had come away with a conclusion: that customers of sports bars preferred sports bars that were a lot of fun. Now, on this Saturday night in September 2003, the Teletech colleagues Carlos Williams and Tyler Jones were enjoying the fruits of that meeting. The sense of mirth at Thirsty's was evidenced not only by the dozen TV sets and the oldies radio station—which now blasted the song "99 Tears"—but also by the sausage-shaped balloons that certain waitresses wore like tails on the backs of their skirts. Owing to their frosty mugs of Milwaukee's Echelon and the playful atmosphere, these two men viewed life's mysteries and challenges in a much lighter light. Helping matters was the pile of nachos on the table below their chins. As each moment passed, the chips and cheese covered less and less of the burgundy platter. They were, the two men agreed, awesome nachos, maybe the best ever.

So it was definitely a fun time. But Carlos still felt a pang every few minutes. Something edgy nagged his mind, and edginess was not his style. Finally, he came out with it.

"Hey Ty, you know, I'm almost glad Adam's not here. I mean, hear me out. I love the guy, but maybe he cramps our style."

Tyler halfway closed one eye and arched the opposing brow. "You mean, he'd impress the girls and we wouldn't?"

Carlos looked down and tried to collect himself before it was too late.

This was tricky terrain. This was not some schmuck he was talking about; this was Adam he was talking about. "Well, you have to admit, he is kinda glib—I mean, when he's not all reticent and faraway and mumbly. And the ladies love guys who are all glib and reticent and, like, faraway and mumbly."

Nodding, Tyler said, "And he cuts a dashing figure, don't you think? Like a soccer player. Ladies just love those foreign soccer players."

Carlos sprang forward, his hands clasped as if in prayer. He blurted, "Do you sometimes find his dimple comforting?" And then he slumped back just as aggressively. "I mean . . . what can I say? If he was here between us, we wouldn't stand a chance. The ladies would look right past us."

"Yeah, but still, I wish he was here," mumbled Tyler. "He's fun, even when he's, like, mumbly and all."

"Well, we've gotta stop dreaming and get down to business. Because without him it's up to us to . . . use our own . . . our own—"

"Devices?"

"Yes!" He slapped the table. "That's the word I'm looking for. It's up to us to use our own devices to procure some skirt."

Terrified by the prospects, Tyler pulled the mug to his mouth and medicated himself thusly.

***

At a mammoth intersection with complicated turn lanes and multiple signals to sit through, Adam shifted his Camry into Park in order to relax his right foot. The air conditioning hummed and a sedate CD played just above a whisper, as if the indy rocker was performing alongside a golf match. On either side of the road stood all sorts of strip malls and stand-alones, as far as the eye could see.

Lori, in the passenger seat, questioned the value of this latest idea.

Adam said, "Hey, you're the product manager. What do you suggest?"

"Project manager. Not product."

"We can't sit still. You even said his car would stand out. Those pinstripes and all. So maybe we'll spot it somehow. I doubt the thing's in his garage on a Saturday night."

"It's gonna take a miracle," she said. "He might not even live out this way. He might be in the city."

"That guy? Down in the city with the minorities and the gals who sleep with other gals. No way."

"Or maybe up north, in Platte County. There's a lotta new wealth up there on the Missouri side."

The light finally turned green. Adam shifted into Drive. "Odds are he's within five miles of us. There's a lotta new subdivisions out this way, and all those high-end apartments and condos." Turning to face Lori, he said, "I mean, I'm just playing the odds. When you play the odds, you end up winning more than losing."

"Adam, this guy's up there's crawling, riding his brakes. We're not getting anywhere out here."

"What can I do? Buggy ain't got wings."

"Okay, let's say he does live around here. Even still, you think we're gonna spot his stupid little sports car? Look around you, fella. There are cars everywhere. My kingdom for a car."

"But they all look the same," he said. "Everywhere you look it's one of those big-ass silver SUVs. There. And there. And there's another."

"Maybe you're right for once. Maybe it's all we can do. And maybe if we're lucky, lady luck will kiss us tonight. What've we got to lose?"

"Three million each," he said conclusively.

"And since we're playing the odds, I guess we should try the big dumb sports bars first. Check out their parking lots. That is, if you can get around this slow-poke in the Escalade. I think his tires have broken legs."

"Actually that's a logical idea," he said, nodding. "Sports bars."

After a rare half-minute of dual silence, she gripped her crown with both hands and said, "Adam, my head is truly swimming. I'd like to fantasize about the cash, you know, and make plans for all the great things it could do. But I'm afraid to get my hopes up. I'm not superstitious, but I've got this nagging sense I'll just jinx it if I make any plans right now."

With a chuckle, he said, "Sounds like all that money's changed you already, huh? Made you superstitious."

"It will not change me. The money will not change me. If we get it, that is." Then, looking into the vague reflection of her face in the side window, she mused about maybe buying a Starbucks franchise.

"Don't tell me you'd waste a single dollar on an idea like that."

She flinched at the venom in his voice. "It would do well. You know it would."

He flopped his head back, a gesture she heard but did not see. She also heard him moan.

"Oh come on, Drama King." Now she faced him. "So you prefer the little independent coffee shops. Hmm, that's a big surprise. You are so noble."

"Well, whatever. Your side has won. That's all I know."

"My side has won? Ha! Who do you think I am? What side am I on? You think I'm some rich big-shot or something? Life's expensive out here, in case you haven't noticed. I live paycheck to paycheck, Adam. I've never had much. Never. Back in college I got scholarships and I still had to work two lousy jobs and I still had to clip coupons like mad. I ate ramen noodles and hot dogs and other cheap, barf-out food that'll probably send me to an early grave. I drove a crappy car that . . . that smelled like . . . like a monster's butt. And I dragged trash bags full of soda cans to the store for cash. One day a street bum ripped the bag right out of my hands and took off. That hobo was fast, even in snow boots." She paused to remember it, shaking her head all the while. When she spoke again, her delivery was different; altered perhaps by the pause itself and the benefits of a deep breath taken, her tone was now, of all things, intimate. "God, this is so intense. The suspense. The helplessness. I mean, I sit here trying to convince myself I don't want that money, just so it won't hurt too much if we fail, but the truth is I do want that money. It's life-changing, Adam. It buys you certain freedoms. You know, I've been through tons of training on how to think outside the box and all of that. How to turn it all upside down and inside out. Hell, I could paper your cubicle with certificates I've earned. I could cover your only sport jacket—the one you dust off for weddings—I could cover the lapels of that sucker with certification pins if I wanted. But right now I cannot come up with a single damned solution for getting those jeans in our hands."

Staring numbly at the stagnant traffic light, Adam let a moment pass. And then he said, "Were you talking to me?"

She roared. The laughter echoed throughout the car and somehow made things too warm in there. It even thawed his cheeks so he could smile more easily. He felt hot air rising through the neckline of his shirt. The tip of his spine tingled, and that tickle descended to the cleft of his ass, and he wiggled a little to see if he could prolong it. Say what you will about this gal, but she's a good laugher, he told himself. The other one, Erin, just happened to be a non-laugher. Whenever Adam said something funny, she'd arch her brows or respond with words: "that's hilarious" or "nice one" or even the dreaded "touché."

Lori cleared her throat and said, "Well, enough about me. So what plans do you have then? With your millions."

"Somehow I'm gonna make things better for the little guys."

She laughed. This time the laughter didn't warm him at all.

"What?" he said, irritated.

"The little guys. Exactly what little guys?"

"You know. The little guys."

"Midgets?"

"You know exactly what I mean. After all, you just described yourself as a little guy. But I'm mostly thinking about the little guys who get bullied by the big shots and the rich guys."

"I bet you some of the big shots and rich guys were little guys once."

"And that's what makes their bad behavior so repellant. Because they should know better. They've been there."

"Oh, Adam. No offense, but when it comes to this, you sort of need to grow up, don't you think?"

"Lori! Seriously? Why does anyone who doesn't celebrate the rich and powerful have to grow up? What a cop out that is. And bad for the world. Worship is precisely what they want from us! Because that way we'll never question what they say and do. They want us to think they're smarter than the rest of us so we'll keep giving 'em tax breaks and bail-outs and second and third chances. Give me a break, please. And it really chaps my ass that so many rich people fell into it by birth or by cheating or by treating people badly."

Watching him with an analyst's eye, she said, "Not to pry, but I've heard things, you know. About recent events in your life. And so there'd be some ironic delight if you got those millions, I'm guessing."

"There would be a certain ironic delight if I got rich after all," he conceded.

"Would you use that cash to win her back?"

"Lori, she's no good. I was barking up the wrong tree. My mistake. She's no damn good."

"That sounds decisive. Harsh even. No gray area there?"

He looked squarely at her. "Deception? Lying? Being drawn to a guy just for his money? Especially Ian Moon of Gerald Moon Motors."

"Wait. You're kidding. She stiffed you for the guy who sucks on the giant pacifier?"

"No, that geezer in the diaper isn't Ian Moon. That geezer is Commander Felix. Ian Moon's the one who sucks on giant dicks."

"Ha. Nice."

"It's his dad who owns all those dealerships. Felix in the diaper does their taxes. But probably not in a diaper. I don't know. Anyway, get a load of this: I tried to take this woman, this Erin, to a quaint little Greek restaurant, a really charming place, nothing phony about it, but I think it spooked her. It didn't look trendy enough, I suppose. So she made up some half-assed lie about having Greek for lunch, and she dragged us to that Remarkable Rib place."

"Oh, that? My sympathies."

"Thank you!"

"Smells great, but even bad barbecue can smell good."

"Yes! Yes! I've actually said the same thing myself. You know, I'd give you a high-five if I was the type of guy who meted out high-fives."

"So where'd you meet her anyway?"

"A gym."

She gave a disparaging nod. "Ah, yes, one of those numbers."

"No, it was the kind of gym that people go to if they want to exercise."

"How many years were you together?" she asked.

"Years? That's a laugh."

"All this trauma, don't tell me it wasn't years."

"Days, Lori. Try days."

Her laughter made Adam's forehead moisten and his cheeks burn. He nudged the volume on the sound system a little bit higher, as if that would make a difference. Soon she wiped an eye with a sidelong thumb and said she'd been under the impression the woman had left him after a very long courtship.

"Well, whatever. It's old news now," he said grumpily. "She goes with a rich guy who rips off senior citizens. How she sleeps at night is beyond me. But what about you, smarty? You went out with that awful Mike Smith."

"Oh lord, you got me there. What can I say?"

"It's me who should be laughing hard now," he said through clenched jaws.

"I can't explain it. That was not my finest hour, Adam. I mean, there was throbbing music, there was liquor, the lighting was dim. I hadn't had a date for a while and so I guess I just panicked. It was strange. And, yes, I'm embarrassed by it now, if that makes you happy. And, yes, it would kill me if that guy got the jackpot. So, enough with the biographies, huh? Back to work."

"Back to work. That's what it feels like, actually. Feels like we might as well be digging holes somewhere and shoveling the dirt right back into 'em."

"You mean the way we keep bickering and trying to outsmart the other?"

"That too."

"Oh. You meant figuring out how to find the guy? Yes. Of course. It's him we need to outsmart, which should be easy. But, damn, it doesn't help that we're just dragging along in this traffic."

"See, here's what gripes me," Adam began, using his free hand to help tell the story. "We're always told that women are so romantic, but they're actually pragmatic. Yes, they enjoy roses and sunsets and scented candles, but when you pull back the curtain, they're mostly just interested in good earners."

"I thought you were done talking about her. Six million bucks is pending."

"Right, but here's the final point I'm going to make and then I'll shut up: we men could not care less how much some woman makes."

"Long as she has nice tits."

"Okay, then, what did you see in that Mike Smith guy anyway?"

"I just told you I don't have an answer for that. Maybe it was the sangrias. Maybe it's that simple. Sometimes the simplest answer is the right answer. And those things, sangrias, do a number on me."

"You had to see something. I mean, guys probably come up to you a lot in bars and stuff."

"They do at that."

"No joke?"

"Are you surprised?"

"No. Not at all. And you don't pay attention to 'em every time, do you?"

She sighed long and loudly. "I suppose if I have to say something, and if it'll shut you up, that doofus seemed ambitious. Confident."

Anyone observing that Camry would've sworn its driver had just suffered a stroke, seeing the way it swerved into the turn lane, veered into the first parking lot, and came to the harshest of stops in the nearest empty space. The whole time, Lori held on to the sides of her seat and gaped at him, her mouth hanging, her brows aloft.

After shifting into Park, he unclicked his safety belt and edged closer, as if to make an impulsive romantic move. He even settled his right fingertips on her shoulder, but lightly, as if upon a Ouija board.

"Adam?" she said.

It's fair to say that neither party was certain if she was questioning a romantic move or inviting it. There was a lot for Lori to analyze in this short, short space of time. Was he only showing how repulsive the traits of confidence and ambition really are? Or, just the opposite: Was he hoping to dazzle her by demonstrating his own confident style?

In an intimate whisper, his eyelashes mere inches from hers, he solved the riddle: "Lori, please listen to this because it's very important and sometimes I think I'm the only guy in the world who actually gets it." He tapped her shoulder twice. "Anyone can be confident. Anyone. It's just a decision, Lori. A choice. And it can easily be faked. It's not a talent like being funny. You cannot choose to be funny, just like you cannot choose to be a baritone or choose to be the fastest runner in the world."

"O-kay," she said, dragging the second syllable.

"It's not even a good thing to choose. Like, kindness would be a good thing to choose. Or humility. Or generosity. In fact, I'd say that confidence is usually a bad thing. Think of the most confident people you know. What good have these loudmouths and braggarts and blowhards really done for humanity? Sure, some are rich now, but what kinds of odious things did they have to do to get there? What kind of useless crap did they foist on us—stuff we don't need and can't afford? Stuff that ends up making us unhappy. How much quality time do they spend with their kids? I could go on and on, but, really, the damn thing is—and I might have buried the lead here—the damn thing is, most guys act all confident just to mask their insecurities and their shortcomings."

"Like, insecurities about their dick size?" she asked with false sincerity.

Adam backed away. "Well, they usually buy big guns to mask that. But, yes, broadly speaking."

"And women are forever deceived by all of this?"

He returned to the posture of a driver, facing forward, his hands on either side of the wheel. "Okay then, what if that Mike Smith just moped around all drag-ass and drove a Pacer? Would he have been so fascinating at that happy hour?"

"About as fascinating as Monique if she weighed two-hundred."

After a burdened sigh, he applied his safety belt in a heavy motion, shaking his head and muttering all the while.

"What?" Lori soon said, her arms folded, her torso twisted in order to face him. Then, more sharply, she demanded: "Say it, Adam. I can handle it."

"I don't know."

"You chicken?"

"Sometimes. But not now."

"Say it then."

"Jesus, relax. I was just gonna say something about romance, I guess. But it doesn't matter now. The moment has passed."

"Chicken."

"Since when do you care what I have to say about anything?"

"Chicken!"

He heaved a sigh. "It's just that if I'd seen you dragging that pathetic bag of soda cans down the street, and then seen a hobo stealing it from you . . . and then seen you chasing him, well . . . ."

"Well what?"

"I might've fallen for you right then and there."

Lori furrowed her brows and kept them creased even as she transitioned to a grin. "You mean you'd root for me over a lovable old hobo in galoshes?"

"Wait-wait-wait!" He fiercely extended an index finger. "Remember now, you'd have been a complete stranger to me and so I couldn't have known what a pain in the ass you are."

Nodding, she said, "Fair enough. Hmm. Hmm."

Her expression was kind of dreamy, he thought, and he wondered if she might follow up with words that were charitable as well, perhaps words about his own rarified charms, but she took a different tack.

"You know, I went and rooted for the hobo in a way. Decent guy, actually. I went and bought him a couple tostados."

"Tostados?" he said.

"You know, those one things. The taco's flattish cousin."

"Well, this is fascinating stuff. Absolutely fascinating. Tostados for hobos." He clapped and then re-applied his hands to the wheel. "Okay, so how about you call the lottery hotline again. Maybe somebody's claimed the money by now and we can get on with our lives."

"You could say please."

He shifted into drive. "Okay. Please then. Please call that hotline, my precious dear. Please, Sweetie, please."

"All right then. When you put it so nicely like that, what other choice do I have?"

***

For a Saturday night in September, the turnout at Thirsty Mack's was disappointing. There was speculation among the staff that karaoke night at The Magnificent Quaff was responsible for thinning their own stack of receipts, but the barmaids did their best to keep smiles on their faces and make their guests feel valued. At a certain table, oblivious to that particular backroom drama, Carlos and Tyler felt valued enough as they sipped from their mugs of Echelon and attacked a second appetizer, Thirsty's sinfully famous Onion Catacombs. And though engrossed in that delicacy, the two men noticed a pair of young women passing by. From behind two sets of spectacles, their four eyes followed the stout young women, who soon selected a table fifteen feet away but perfectly within the fellows' line of sight. These new guests went by the names Bertie and Lida. Bertie was a dirty blonde and Lida an occasional redhead, and this night was such an occasion. They wore heavy lipstick, pullover tee-shirts, patchy blue jeans, and black boots that terminated in rings of fur at mid-calf.

"You see that?" Carlos whispered.

His mouth full, Tyler nodded vigorously.

"Two plus two equals four," said Carlos.

"And, dammit, we would be eating onions."

As Bertie straddled her stool and settled in for the ride, she smiled at the guys a moment longer than most women would.

***

As Adam Durham snailed along in dense traffic, he noticed a patrol car in an oncoming lane. Long ago his dad had a flirtation with police scanners, perhaps hoping to hear the mayor or the bishop get arrested for something lurid. Adam now recalled how the radio had constantly run names and addresses through the crime computer. He asked Lori if she knew any cops who could help them out by providing access to that superhuman computer. The answer was no.

"Me neither," he said. "Which is a good thing because I'm not at my best around figures of authority. Men in uniforms. Men with pistols. Men with arbitrary power." He might have given more background on this facet of his life—and on the twisted influence of Crazy Hubie—but time was short, tongues were tart, nerves were shot, and what the hell did it matter anyway?

She said, "No sweat. I'd do all the talking. In fact, I bet you I can sweet-talk a cop into digging up that address for us."

"Really?"

"I have a way."

"Since when?"

"Piece of cake."

"Okay then, how can we make this happen? Is it worth making a bogus call to 9-1-1? Like, is that a federal crime or something?"

"I guess we just wait to find a cop and go from there. Jesus, like right there!" She pointed at a patrol car parked near a defunct yogurt stand, a lone vehicle in an isolated lot. "Look. It's just sitting there, waiting for us. How about that? Our luck is changing, Adam!"

He'd never spoken to a real cop before. Now the poor guy's bowels began churning. He hoped the churning didn't get too loud or too urgent.

"Let's do this," she said, wringing her palms. "Get in the turn lane! Now! The clock is ticking!"

Before long, Adam's window was equal to that of the officer's window, with the cars facing opposite directions. The cop was a handsome black man who looked barely old enough to vote. He strained for a better view of Lori as he asked them what was up.

Adam waited for Lori behind him to do all the talking, as she'd promised, but it was turning out to be a broken promise. So he said, "Uh, I mean, there's this guy we know, Mike Smith, and he's acting all strange."

Eying Adam now, the young cop said, "Wait, are you okay? You seem kinda worked up."

His voice cracked, puberty style: "Me? I'm great. Thanks. Pretty good. Super. And you?"

The cop leaned out the window at an angle and called past him, to Lori. "This kid on weed or something?"

She pushed closer to the driver's side and cleared her throat, as if to pre-empt any puberty creaks of her own. "Him? Uh, he has a speedy metabolism."

"Ah. Okay. Whew, I'm gettin' too old for this." The officer's left hand, which had been dangling out the window, now slapped the car door. "So, acting strange, you say. Why don't you let me tell you about my day." He now displayed four fingers and a thumb. "Five minutes ago, I was trying to reason with a strange guy. Seems this party was under the belief that Satan was living within his sofa. You hear me right? So, what did he do about it?" He paused, his brows arched, as if awaiting guesses. "I'll tell you what he did. This gentleman went ahead and started that sofa on fire. Now how about that? Trying to burn Satan. You ever hear such a thing? Might as well try to drown a fish. Anyway, you can smell the smoke on my arms." He gave one a sniff. "So I suggest you take a deep breath and back up and tell me about this friend that's acting strange. Is he a threat to others or to himself? And keep your answer succinct because it's been a long, long day."

Adam's mouth opened, but no words came out. After two sludgy seconds he turned. "Lori? A little help here."

She edged even closer to Adam's window, placing her left hand on his right shoulder for leverage. "Uh, we just saw him, uh, behind that store over there. He was acting strange. Right, Adam? Near his little Porsche. Cherry-red with pinstripes."

Nodding madly, Adam said, "She's right about the Porsche."

"Look, folks, I've been awake since nine a.m., and I know there's weird stuff in the world, and I could give you examples that'd scare you bad. All right? So now that I've got your attention, tell me what exactly was this party doing."

Looking back and forth from the cop to Lori, Adam said, "He was, like, rolling a bowling ball down the middle of the street? Right?"

Lori's eyes widened from disbelief, but she managed to nod.

"Hmm, that does qualify as strange. A bowling ball? Hmm. Very strange. This has been the day from hell. First Satan and now a bowling ball. Do you have a description?"

"Black and round," said Adam.

Reaching for a notepad, the cop said, "Black and round. Wait, black and round? For God's sake, not the bowling ball. You're sittin' over there killin' me, guy."

"Oh! Of course. Sorry! You mean I should describe Mike Smith."

The officer slapped the car door again, but harder this time. "Miss, why don't you do the talking now? From the top, but succinct."

Lori leaned outward, smiled a twitchy grin, cleared her throat again, and placed her fingertips below both ears as if to steady her jaws for the tough task ahead. "Okay, his name is Mike Smith. He's thirty-five or forty. Blond I guess but balding fast. He goes six-two, I'd say. Husky now, but he'll be a fat pig pretty soon. Sorry, nothing against pigs. Not that you're a pig. I mean, you know what I mean. Well, I mean he carries himself like a total doofus is what I'm trying to say, like a big shot or something. And if there's a way you can match him up with his car—that Porsche I mentioned—then you can probably get his home address pretty quickly, right? And they'll say it over the radio thing you've got. Right?"

"Hold the phone, Miss. Something's going on here. You two are awful nervous and now you seem awful eager to get this party's address. Now why do I get the feeling you hope to find this guy so you can tee-pee his yard? If I inspect your vehicle, will I find all kinds of toilet paper? Because if I do, it's all going home with me. It's been that kinda day."

Mercifully, the emergency double tones on his radio interrupted things. The officer extended a flat hand as if to silence the two taxpayers.

"Strong-armed robbery in progress," said a dispatcher, "in the parking lot of Optimum Surgical Supplies, 556 Matador Way."

"What a day! Looks like I won't be tossing your car tonight, folks. Chalk it up to good luck! Very good luck indeed! Tonight's your lucky night!" The officer donned his hat with his right hand even as the tires of his patrol started to screech.

Adam and Lori watched the Crown Vic lay some righteous rubber.

"I told you our luck was turning," she said.

***

Inside Gino's Gentlemen's Club, two muscular gentlemen in black satin jumpsuits lifted Mike Smith by either of his armpits. "Next time keep those grubby hands to yourself or we'll be happy to chop 'em off," advised one of the men. En route to the doorway, his heels strafing the carpet, Mike Smith rotated his neck and stole one last look at the ladies on stage before he got sent reeling onto the pavement outside.

Quickly he found his feet. He was a little wobbly but recalled where he'd parked because it was such a primo spot right there in the front row. But his car was not there! Instead he saw some lame-ass Jeep with a cellophane window and a hundred hippie bumper stickers! Mike Smith turned in all four directions. He backed up. He went forward. He went forward some more. Finally he collapsed sideways upon the front fender of that sorry Jeep. He punched in 9-1-1 and then he punched the hood of the jeep.

"Listen," he soon said into his phone, "some bastards stole my Porsche. And I know who did it."

***

Adam Durham and Lori Nelson had become so bereft of ideas and so desperate for progress that they resumed scanning the parking lots of big sports bars in the hopes of spotting that little sports car.

"Thirsty's," Adam said coldly as he turned into the same parking lot from where he last spoke with Erin Patterson, by phone, ten days earlier as she prepared to shower for her evening out with the charlatan Ian Moon—the lot for the same sports bar that now sheltered his work buddies Carlos and Tyler, who were engaged in an adventure of their own therein. "Has it come to this?"

"What?"

"The circle of life."

"I don't get you."

"Thirsty's. This is probably where it all gets resolved. Destiny. The circle of life."

"How so?"

"Oh . . . nothing. Never mind. It's a long story."

"You are weird. That cop was right."

As he neared the parking spot from which he'd made that fateful call to Erin, he expected to feel something: a bowel-heavy anxiety, maybe, or despair, or possibly naked hatred. But he felt nothing. In fact, he felt like smirking, so he smirked.

"Now what?" Lori asked, noticing the smirk. "This circle of life is amusing?"

"You don't miss a trick."

"It's just that you're smirking really big, like you're in a skit or something."

"Nothing." He didn't want to talk about Erin Patterson again, so he pretended to be smirking at the Hummer that occupied the very parking space in question. He pointed at it.

She said, "Hey, it's probably Mike Smith's second car. He would have a Hummer, wouldn't he?"

"Every asshole with a few bucks and self-esteem issues has a Hummer these days." But the whole cosmic aspect of it suddenly chilled him: It probably is Mike Smith's Hummer, he told himself, owing to its location, right there in that historic spot. Life can sometimes be weird that way. The circle of life, that is.

"Wait," Lori said. "Missouri plates. No go. No way Mike Smith lives on the Missouri side."

"Just a while ago you said he might live up north, in Platte County. That's Missouri."

"Why would he be way down here? There are plenty of big sports bars up north. You don't have to drive thirty miles for potato skins. This is America."

"Well, true, true," he said, eager to get away from there. "So I guess we're done here. Good riddance. What now?"

"Maybe next we visit the parking lot of some restaurant that sells a lot of meat."

***

Deep inside that same bar and grill, the stakes were high because Adam's cube neighbors were on the business end of furtive glances from the playful Bertie, who was making sexy faces and shifting on her stool a lot, as if the stool had naughty fingers; and from the harlequin-haired Lida, who blew feeble smoke rings and fluttered her eyelashes; she looked both boozy and startled at once, much like the older version of Lucille Ball. Carlos and Tyler responded with Muppet-styled grins before burying their faces into the drink menu.

Carlos covered his mouth with the colorful placard and said, "They're pretty large gals."

Tyler nodded. "Somebody once told me fat girls make the best lovers."

"Who told you that?"
"This fat girl I knew."

***

From a corner booth inside a waffle shop an acre or two up the slope from Gino's Gentlemen's Club, Mike Smith dumped a lot of sugar into his steaming coffee as the waitress, Misty, scratched his order onto her tiny notepad.

"Misty, huh?" he said, sloshing the coffee around to liquefy the sugar. "Name like that, you're supposed to be workin' the pole down the hill there at Gino's."

"It's my true name, sir," she began, with the practiced politeness a service worker is spoon-fed in a two-hour seminar. "I happened to get named after somebody important. Now, down there, in that place, if a girl's named Misty, it's probably just one of them fake names, like, like Desiree maybe, or Josephine."

Having just come from that place down there and its smorgasbord of boobs, butts, and beavers, Mike Smith had an appetite for things saltier than the pigs-in-a-blanket he'd just ordered. Well, this Misty was not much, but she did have a C-plus to B-minus rack and her legs weren't bowed or anything, and she wasn't pigeon-toed or anything in the slightest. Her posture was passable, despite some roundness to the shoulders. But that face. There was something about her face that reminded him of Gomer Pyle, and not in a good way. Otherwise, boy, he'd really throw a fuck into her.

"Be right back with your pigs," she said, turning to go.

"Speakin' a pigs, had to call up the cops because a coupla' dumbshits stole my Porsche tonight."

Porsche? She took a closer gander at the guy. He might have looked wealthy. He did look drunk. To her experience, the worst tippers were the wealthy-looking men, drunk or otherwise, but she still had a hard time believing that to be the case. If I was rich, I'd tip like crazy and enjoy every minute of it, she might say to herself while scraping a few cold coins into her apron.

"Stole your car? You don't say?" she replied tenderly, hoping this fellow with the pinwheel eyes, the hairy arms, and the Gino's ink stamp on the top of his wrist would be an exception to the rule and leave some folding money beside his dirty dishes.

"Yeah, well," he mumbled, bored with her already. He gazed absently out the window. From his vantage point, Mike Smith could not see the front Gino's, which included the first row of parking spaces where his car should have been. But he leaned and leaned just to make sure. "Hey, cops said it could be a few hours before they even get here. A few hours! Where are my tax dollars going?"

"They must be out catchin' murderers. But, yeah, I hear yuh, babe."

***

If the police had not been so busy catching murderers, they might have been there to stop the Porsche 911 after it cruised through a red stoplight on a sleepy two-lane in southern Johnson County. Nate Walker, the driver, would never ignore a red light on purpose, especially while commanding a very hot car, but the man's mind was jumping from place to place. It kept coming back to one rotten place: Without the cash from Harvey, his pockets felt naked, and Florina would be keen to digging some dough from those pockets when he got home. He thought about pawning the Porsche on his own, but Harvey kept the names of the good bad guys under lock and key in order to prevent such straying from the program, and it was too dangerous to start fishing for fencers. So Nate was left with no choice but to put the Porsche back where he'd gotten it, fetch his own van from a nearby lot, and chalk the whole thing up as a lesson. Actually, except for the gas he'd wasted, the time he'd wasted, and the noxious ribbing he'd gotten at the shop, the experience had been a total kick.

***

While Mike Smith was making do with the final shards of sausage on his plate, he failed to notice a gray Tempo returning to Gino's parking lot, carrying two determined men, each with his game face on. The car soon entered a parking space that faced the strip joint but was neither close to the building nor far from it. Way up front, the spot that once held the Porsche and later the Jeep with the hippie stickers was again empty.

"So, we just wait for him to come out?" asked Scotty from the passenger seat.

"It was your idea, remember? But how do we even know he's still in there when there's no car to tip us off? He coulda' called a taxi or anything. Man, you just had to make me stop for hamburgers and slow us down."

"I was hungry."

"Right, and now it's been long enough, he coulda' gone home. Man, we need to peek inside."

"Fobb, you figure out how to peek inside a nudie bar, and we bottle that shit and sell tickets."

Frustrated, the twerp placed both hands on Scotty's left shoulder and gave a gentle nudge. "You go in then. See if he's still in there. Go ahead."

"Me? Why me?"

"I refuse to pay a cover. It's like paying good money at a restaurant where they let you look over the food and smell it but don't let you eat."

Scotty did not exit the Tempo, but he did lean forward because something strange was happening in that front row of parked cars. In fact, what he saw was so ridiculous that his voice got as high-pitched as a schoolgirl's: "Dude, what the hell?"

Together they saw a cherry-red Porsche 911 with pinstripes glide into the very same spot that Mike Smith had chosen earlier that night! The driver, the same flashy fellow in clashing colors they'd spied earlier, now unfolded himself from the driver's side, shut the door, and casually strolled away.

Fabrizio declared his world no longer made sense.

"Maybe he was just cleaning it like I said a while back. Bein' it's the same guy and all," Scotty offered as they watched the figure disappear.

"I don't know, man. Nothin' adds up."

"The slacks looked different. Checkers all over the place, but still different," said Scotty. "You know, it's like somebody's jackin' with us on purpose. We gotta figure this out, Fobb. But first I really need to pee. I can't concentrate while the back of my teeth are swimmin'."

"You think I'm stoppin' you? Go. It'll give me time to figure this shit out."

"Where?"

"Step outside. It's dark. Who cares? Just don't go pissin' on the tire again. Last time I had to scrub and scrub."

"All right. But I take very long pees, remember? So it could be a while. I mean, I can hold it and hold it and then . . . timmmm-berrrrr!"

"Go!"

"And remember how I get piss-shy real easy, Fobb? So do me a solid and don't watch."

In a seething tone, Fabrizio said, "Listen, just take your sweet time because this whole night has basically blown my mind and I need some peace and quiet to think it all over. I can't think straight with you there breathin' all next to me. So take your time. Have a blast. Now go!"

"Ten-four, good buddy."

Meanwhile uphill, the burly source of their struggles shifted in the booth until he was positioned more sideways than not, in the pose of a prom queen. From this angle, through the trees Mike Smith could more clearly see Gino's back doors, and he hoped one or two of the strippers would step outside topless to have a smoke. He'd love to catch a thrill for free. He deserved at least that much. In fact, he had half a mind to sue those fuckers for tossing him out like that. His eyes then drifted across the parking lot and soon settled on an interesting sight: a fellow whizzing high into the night sky. It was an impressive stream, one that caught the county's ambient light and looked sort of artful, even to him. Less impressive was the dumpy figure, the purveyor of the piss stream, who was swaying in the fashion of a blind soul singer.

Mike Smith grabbed for his phone.

Inside the Tempo, Fabrizio answered the call and heard this: "You dumb wop bastard, I want my car."

"Hey! It's you! Wait a minute because—"

"Done waiting, dumb-ass."

"Look, we never took your car. And besides—"

"Surprised you'd have the sack to do such a thing. But I'm ready to go ballistic. So get it back to me or else."

"Honest. Someone else took your car."

He pounded the table with the side of his fist, which drew concerned looks from customers and employees alike, including a uniformed security guard, and so he tempered his voice to a low growl. "Return it now. And it best be in primo shape or you and that dumb-ass Irish Mick will have hell to pay."

"I said we didn't take your car. Some black dude took it. Had to be a pro, he got in and out so fast."

"You're a terrible liar. Blaming black guys. And a bigot. How predictable."

"No. I swear it. I'm not a bigot or nothin'. I swear it. But the big news is, this thief even brought your car back a minute ago. To the very same spot even. Don't ask me why."

"Stop shittin' me. I know where you live. Matter of fact, I could kick both your asses in two minutes. So tell your fat buddy in the Elvis Grbac jersey down there to put his dick in his pants before I cram it inside his mouth."

Fabrizio dropped the phone onto his lap, opened his door, and leaned on it. "Hurry man."

"You told me to go slow."

"Shake it off and get in! Now!"

"I'm gettin' some mixed signals here."

"He's close, Scotty. Mike Smith is close. He just called. He knows you got your dick in your hands."

"What makes you think he's close?"

***

Having failed to find the Porsche in Thirsty Mack's parking lot, Adam and Lori returned to the commercial roads, where they once again decayed with a million other sputtering vehicles on a warm Saturday night in September. Likewise, things inside the car had gone musty as well. At least, that's how Lori saw it. After several minutes of unprecedented silence, she said, "Adam?"

Dreamily, he went "Hmm?"

"You sleepy?"

"Not especially."

"You've stopped wiggling."

"Me?"

"You've stopped clearing your throat. You've stopped drumming your fingers on stuff. You've stopped doing that thing with your neck. You're actually holding still for once."

"Yeah? Crap, I had no idea."

"So what's up?"

"It's all good," he said with a lilt.

She slapped the console between them. "You're giving up! That's it, right?"

He laughed.

"You're basking in the relief of surrender!"

He laughed again.

"Talk to me."

He smiled.

"Talk to me! Tell me what's going through that head of yours?"

He flattened his back upon the back-rest and stretched his arms so that both hands were atop the steering wheel. He sensed it was the right posture to use when delivering interesting information. "Okay. Whatever. It's just that two minutes ago, give or take, I got hit with this epiphany. Suddenly I realized, in this flash of enlightenment, this moment of truth, that I'm never getting that money. Because, you know, guys like me don't get things like that. And the beauty of it is, I don't care. I don't even care. I feel fine."

Lori was not the type to roll her eyes; she considered it a trite and predictable gesture done by the inarticulate ones among us. But now she rolled her eyes.

"If you think about it," he continued, looking at her instead of the road, "those millions would just turn me into the kind of guy I despise."

"Now I've heard everything."

"I feel like such a phony for even wanting that dough. But we've had fun, haven't we? It's been a wild ride. The journey's what really matters."

Lori's laugh quickly turned scornful. "The journey? Give me a break. Journey? You're wimping out and trying to rationalize it all. You're giving up because it's the easy way out. Because you're afraid to care too much about anything that might fail."

"Hey folks, we've got Dr. Joyce Brothers over here!"

"Man, the psychology of this is so simple. You invested your heart and soul into that woman and—"

"Woman? I'm talking about the jackpot."

"However you care to refer to her."

"Clever," he said.

"No, it was that woman, Adam. And it didn't work out. And you're not ready for another dose of pain. Hey, I get it. Half the movies out there have that same exact theme. So don't try to put one past me."

"You're jumping to wild conclusions."

"No, that's what's going on. And . . . look, I'm not mad. I get it, okay? It's human nature. But, gosh, what can I say? I guess I don't have any wise sayings to fix everything. I don't have any inspirational calendars at home to draw from."

"That's a surprise."

"For real? You think I'm into things like that? New Age stuff?"

"I guess I mean corporate culture stuff, which is just as dopey. You know, personal growth as defined by the stiffs who make up Corporate America. Marketing consultants. The 'wow' factor. Sizzle this and sizzle that. Or whatever. I don't know. I'm getting tired."

"Ha! You don't know. You don't know what you're talking about, Adam. That's not me. And just so you know, smart guy, my sister gets me a calendar for Christmas every year. And every year I use it, whether I hate it or not, because I happen to love her. This year it was called '12 Big Hunks From the Big 12.' And none of those hunks have had an inspirational thing to say so far. Which is neither here nor there. So, I don't know. What can I say?"

"You'll think of something."

"But I get it. I get it." She slugged his shoulder. In a more plaintive tone, she said, "Anyway, let's just go for it. Keep on keepin' on, huh? You and me. There's nothing to fear."

"You could actually do this without me."

"But . . . we're a team, huh?"

"A couple of unlikely teammates," he muttered.

"Who cares? It doesn't matter if we're different or not. We're complementary, maybe."

"Like how?"

"Well . . . hmm. I guess my strengths, coupled with your weaknesses, give us a good balance or something. Anyway, forget that. I know what. Let's call this a rallying cry and get back to work because you'd make better use of that money than Mike Smith or some other jackass, and so would I. He'd just end up buying more rich-guy toys that make the rich guys richer. And then other rich guys would see those big-ass toys and so they'd have to go buy their own bigger-ass toys, and, well, it's a vicious cycle, I guess."

"Lori, my goodness, you're starting to sound like me."

She flopped back but just as quickly leaned forward again. "Look, one last rallying point and then it'll be my turn to shut up: In life, it's kind of true when they say the good things don't come easy. Most of the time you have to work for 'em. They just cost more, in effort or money or whatever."

"Tell that to Ian Moon," he grumbled.

"Adam! Exactly what good has come to him? He's stuck with that shallow Erin! Have you ever thought of it that way?"

In the style of a slow burn, Adam turned to face his passenger. He then tore both hands from the wheel and tried to make a touchdown signal, but the car was way too small. "Yes! Ha! Yes, you're right, Lori. Thank you. It feels so good to hear it. What you said, I mean. Because it's true. He's got to deal with her. You've gone and rallied me!"

"Are you messing with me?"

"I'm stoked. Really."

"You're not pulling my leg?"

"No. Honest."

"You're not all of a sudden demented because of what we've been through tonight?"

"No. I'm great!"

"No sugar imbalances or anything like that, because it's been a long time since we've had any carbs and sometimes mood swings can—"

"I'm cool. It's all great. Slap me some five!"

Lori shrugged and then shouted "whoo-hoo!" It was a lot like the "whoo-hoo!" hollered by young women when they expose their tits in public.

Smiling, the driver looked again at the road and did that thing with his neck again and asked what comes next.

"Hell if I know. But we're stoked, right? And so together we'll figure something out."

"Yeah, but to tell you the truth, I've always hated that word. Stoked."

"Me too! Me too! Man, we're on a roll!"

***

Mere moments earlier, while the thrills of revenge chilled the blood that already iced his veins, Mike Smith had witnessed the panicked departures of the two amateurs in that grotesque gray Tempo. Now he swaggered downhill through a greenspace and two parking lots on his way to wait for the cops in front of Gino's. In fact, as he peered into his cell phone with the plan to call the police and harass them into hurrying, he nearly bumped into his own car! The beloved Porsche 911 was precisely where he'd left it two or three hours ago, just as Fabrizio had told him. He cupped his hands at the driver's window and saw his key-ring on the driver's seat. He then dug into his pants pocket and felt the back-up key he'd had to use when he left home that evening. He backed against his car and took pause. Something is weird, he said to himself. Did some dick-wipe slip me a Mickey at Gino's?

Well, in any regard, his car was back and his belly full. The world was once again spinning on its axis in the ways his God intended. Now he could concentrate on getting laid.

***

On a neighborhood back road, safely distant from Mike Smith and from the flashy thief in checkered slacks, Fabrizio Leone had the time to tell Scotty O'Connor about the threats he'd gotten over the phone.

"He said all that? Irish Mick and wop and what else?"

"Dumb-ass. Or else dumbshit," he replied, scratching at his purple stocking cap. "Either way, they're both insulting."

"Fobb, he may have crossed the line this time. I mean, I'm just sayin'."

"Man, I know. We can't just let this go. How much longer we gonna let folks shit all over us? Sometimes I think in life you gotta fight back."

Scotty made two fists but let them drop on his thighs. "I'm so mad I could pound his ass into submission."

"Would you do that? You're kinda big, I mean."

"Oh I would. You know I would."

Fabrizio nodded as he flicked on his turn signal. "We're goin' back. You and me. Nobody treats us like that and gets away with it forever."

***

Inside Thirsty's, Carlos Williams grabbed his friend's shoulder as if the home team had just scored a winning basket at the buzzer. The move was noisy, heavy, and obvious to anyone watching, including the two stout women across the way, but the poor guy could not help it.

"Look, Ty!" he began in an unflattering fusion of a whisper and a squeal. "They keep looking at us."

"Shh, I know it," Tyler mumbled, his head down.

"We've got to do something. If we don't do something, we'll hate ourselves the rest of our lives."

"I could live with that," whispered Tyler.

"No, let's put ourselves out there, bro. Let's take a chance. We've got nothing to lose."

"I don't know. I'm so nervous. What could we even do?"

"We'll have drinks sent over. That always works."

"You've done that?"

"Dummy, on TV it always works. Come on. You with me?"

Looking paler than usual, Tyler said, "But they're having imported beers. See the size of those cans?"

"The way I see it, money's no object at a time like this," advised Carlos as they continued their intense huddle. "We can always get money. We might even win the lottery someday. But these gals—a chance like this may never come again."

From her distance, Lida smiled at them again, and followed it with one slow nod.

Carlos said, "This looks serious. Very serious." He clutched Tyler's shoulder again. "Wait. Before it's too late, we better be proactive and decide who gets which girl."

"Okay. Yeah. I'll go ahead and call dibs on the good-lookin' one."

"Yeah? Okay, I guess. Which one is that?"

***

Already that night, the gray Tempo had covered dozens of miles in its trips to and from Gino's, but on this particular journey it hosted the kind of analysis that would make a think-tank look sick. Only in this case the analysis took place silently, within Fabrizio's brain, for he knew tough decisions had to be made in a hurry, and he knew it was his job to make them, owing to the fact that his business partner was a boob. Nearing Gino's parking lot, he tapped the brakes to slow things.

"I been thinkin'."

"What?" asked his passenger, hopeful. "We pussin' out?"

"Don't put it that way. Makes it sound like we're pussies. But I been thinkin' about how maybe we get somebody a lot tougher than us to beat the tar outta him? For efficiency's sake at least."

"He is a big guy," said Scotty.

"Okay, it's good we talked about this. It's decided then. For tonight we just stick to the plan we started out with and find out where the jag-off lives. Then we let one of our henchmen get him later."

"We don't have any henchmen, do we?"

"We'll find us a real bad dude. Lenny Buck might know someone. Matter of fact, Scotty, who was that one tough bastard on his bowling team? Looked like Herman Monster."

"Can you be more specific?"

"Come on, that one guy. Drove that weak-ass Monza."

"The green one?" asked Scotty.

"Green man or green Monza?" asked Fabrizio.

"Monza."

"Yeah, it was puke green."

Nodding, Scotty said, "Yeah, I remember it now. That guy. The dude they called 'Frankenstein.' I totally forgot about him."

"I wonder what happened to him."

"He sold out. I heard he sold out."

Fabrizio nodded. "Not too surprised. Well, anyway, Lenny Buck knows a lotta other bad bastards. Let's plan on gettin' in touch with him real soon."

***

Within the northernmost quadrant of Thirsty Mack's, the investment in free drinks paid off quickly, for two young women now sat across from Carlos and Tyler, barely an arm's length distant. Even better, in a gesture that was meant to make everyone more at ease, the women beckoned the waitress and ordered another round for themselves.

Bertie said, "Thanks again for all the beers, boys. They're tasty."

"Alcohol's going right to my head," Lida revealed, slanting her chin to the ceiling and fluttering her eyes.

Carlos and his best friend liked the sound of that!

***

Had the rhythm of the traffic lights worked in his favor, Fabrizio Leone might have made it back to Gino's Gentlemen's Club before Mike Smith and his Porsche could get away forever. Such fortune, too, would've given Fabrizio and Scotty the chance to follow the man to his home. Once armed with his address, they could then dispatch a tough son of a bitch to shake him down someday, at the right time. But the sad reality was this: The Tempo entered Gino's parking lot on the south side just as the Porsche was exiting it from the north.

Scotty lurched forward, pointing. "There he goes! Don't lose him! Turn! That way! That way!"

Fabrizio spun the steering wheel and stomped the gas but screeched to a halt. A parade of geese was crossing in front of his car.

"What the hell? At this hour?" He glared at Scotty, wishing to blame the spectacle on him. Then he lowered his window in a fury and cupped his hands around his mouth. "Use your wings, you snotty birds. Fly! Fly!"

Pointing frantically, Scotty said, "Dude's gettin' away! Back up fast!"

"I'm no good at backing up fast!"

"Then honk the damn horn at least!"

"Honk? At geese? What are you thinkin'? That's like barkin' at dogs. They'll just think you want to chit-chat."

***

So far, Mike Smith had led a fairly charmed life, and this evening was no exception. The lucky fellow met with green light after green light and was soon beyond the reach of the sputtery gray Tempo that now pursued him. At the first red traffic light, he played the message that had blinked on his phone for a while. Into his ear came Lori Nelson's voice, in a corny, twisted accent that made him cock a brow: "Hey, Mike. This here's Lori-Lori. Nelson. So sorry about last night. I'd really like to kiss all y'all's privates. All night long. So call me right away, y'all. Uh . . . okay then."

He said, "Desperate skank."

After playing the message a second time, he told himself, let's do this. So he deigned to return the phone call. But the phone call did not make it through because at that same moment Lori Nelson was checking for voice messages that might have been left on her landline phone at home; it was Saturday night, after all. As a consequence, Mike Smith's incoming call went straight to her cell phone's voice mail, which displeased him greatly.

Feigning sadness, Lori said to Adam, "No messages on the home phone. So nobody loves me." She dropped the phone onto her lap.

***

At Thirsty Mack's, the Teletech men had finally, delightfully, loosened up and were making good time with Bertie and Lida, who were drinking sportily and laughing at just about all of their best lines. Young Carlos, emboldened by the beer, spoke amusingly of the time he'd mistaken cabbage for lettuce and therefore made a salad that was "actually pretty awful." Tyler gave a merry account of the time he ate too many multicolored marshmallows and heaved a multicolored mess onto his bed overnight. To this day, he said, he lacks an appetite for the things, "though the white ones can still be awesome." But matters took a weighty turn once the fellows completed a riff on how heartless their workplace had become.

Lida spoke first. She was duly irate. "A one-percent raise is all you got? And the CEO got how much?"

"Millions, I'm sure," answered Tyler. "Plus, they might throw out our casual Fridays."

"Your jobs do sound awful."

"I'd quit in a New York second," Bertie said.

"Right," added Lida. "Doesn't that sound brave, Bertie? Just up and quitting?"

"Legendary! It would rock the joint!"

"Like something from the sixties," said Lida. "Rebellion and all."

Bertie raised her hands and drove a pretend-motorcycle. "Easy Rider, huh? Vroom-vroom."

Carlos said, "We got this really cool friend named Adam that sits by us. You all should meet him sometime. He's like amazing with words and a really good designer, but they've got him doing PowerPoints."

"Poor Adam," said Lida.

"And he said he feels like a bag of Munchos," added Tyler.

"I hear yuh," said Bertie. "Wait, wait." She stuck her cigarette between her lips and reached for her purse. After some ferocious digging, she found her phone and gave it to Tyler, despite the fact that his own phone was within his reach. “Okay, call your boss right now. Both of you. Stick it to The Man.”

“Really?” he said, smiling in case this was all a wonderful joke.

“Really!”

“But what if The Man is a woman?”

Lida got her phone and slid it to Carlos. “You too. Case closed. Finito!”

“It’s Saturday night,” said Tyler. “I mean, off hours and all.”

“Then quit by voice mail. How cool is that? You’ll be legendary.”

The women stared expectantly at the men.

Quietly, to his friend, Carlos said, “Adam has been thinking of quitting.”

***

After surveying yet another parking lot of yet another popular sports bar, Adam and Lori whimpered in unison. They’d been whimpering a lot for a while, halfway to amuse the other, and halfway because they both sort of wanted their mommies.

“You know, we might be doing it all wrong,” she said. “Inefficiently, I mean. The Japanese would go about this very differently. They would have us split up.”

“I’ve done enough splitting up lately.”

“Ha. Well, I’m just saying if we use two cars we can cover twice the ground.”

“You mean, like, you in your car and me in this one?” Adam said.

“I guess that's how it might go.”

“Won't you get lonesome?”

“Me?” She placed her palms on her chest, unsure if he was joking. “I mean, I suppose we’d keep in touch through our phones. As needed. For progress updates and all. And, of course, to make sure we were avoiding duplication of effort.”

“Right. Duplication of effort. Okay. I mean, if you think it's best to head all the way back to Deer Creek to get your car and do this, then I guess who am I to stand in the way?”

“Deer Run. But wait,” she said, reaching, “before we do anything rash, I’ve got this very strange hunch that I should check the lottery hotline again.”

“I don’t like the sound of this hunch.”

But when she took out her phone she saw the message light blinking. She held it out for Adam to see. It lit up the car like a warning light.

“A message!” he shouted, nearly ramming the back fender of a PT Cruiser. “Play it! Put it on hands-free so I can hear!”

“What if it’s personal?”

“Get real.”

It turned out the message was meant to be personal, technically speaking, but Lori didn't treat it that way once she realized it was from the dreaded Mike Smith, the blackguard who stood in the way of their fortunes. Clearly his phone had been losing power or else losing its signal when he'd recorded the message because his words got fainter and fainter with each syllable: "You called, eh? Knew you would. No biggie. Shit happens. Listen, this time why don't you drop by my humble abode? Like, soon. Say, at 11 or so? Got everything we need, including a buttload of wine coolers, which I keep around for the ladies, plus Dolby, and two big screens. Oh, yeah, hope you don't got any bush down there. So, yeah, come on by. I'm at . . . ." and the signal was totally gone.

Adam extended a palm for a sarcastic high-five, which she ignored. He said, "Well, it's nice to know he's got a buttload of wine coolers, and Dolby, and a couple big-ass screens. And it was very nice to learn he prefers a smooth mons veneris." His volume now rose dramatically. "But not so nice that we learned those details at the expense of his goddamn address."

Thinking in practical terms, Lori said, "Wouldn't he know his battery died in mid-sentence? And then wouldn't he get a charger or something and call again to make sure I got the directions?"

"Yeah, probably. I don't know much about these devices, but it could've been some other malfunction, something to do with cell towers or sun spots or moon spots or who knows what, and so he probably has no idea."

Lori threw back her head and placed a fist over each eye. "Did you hear the sleaze in his voice? He thinks I actually want him. It makes my stomach hurt."

"He's a scumbag. At least I can enjoy—we can enjoy—knowing he's gonna be disappointed in the end."

"Meaning?"

"Meaning he won't get to be with you. Obviously."

Instead of confirming his assumption, which of course would've been unnecessary, she shut her eyes and said, "I guess I should call him back and try to get his address. Maybe he's charging the battery or whatever."

But now her phone beeped.

"Another message?" Adam asked, brows elevated.

"Nope. Shit. My battery's dead too. Man, it must be a sign. We're about sunk, I'd say."

"No, not this. Not this. My God. What next? Do we get your phone on a charger? Or do we dare use my phone?"

There was now an edge to her tone. "I don't know. He won't answer if it's your number. Or probably won't, anyway. We've been through all this, remember? I mean, I don't know. I guess I could use it to leave a message, I guess, and maybe ask for his address. Not that he'd even play that message if it comes from your phone number. Or maybe he would play it. I guess I've been wrong before. I guess—"

"Actually, no! Skip it."

"Why?"

"Because it's getting to you. Which makes sense because he's awful and you're not. All I know is I'd love you to never set eyes on that guy again, not even to trick him."

"But I guess he might answer," she said, softly, tiredly. "I mean, I know I'm speaking out of both sides of my mouth, but we're so close. I could buck up and leave another message."

"I'd rather you didn't."

She looked at him for a long moment.

"It kind of makes my stomach turn to hear you, like, sweet-talk that brute," he said in a whisper. "I hate for guys like that to have even a moment's delight."

"Adam, I'm okay."

"You are?"

"Emotions can sometimes erupt, but in the end . . . I mean, we can put up with some temporary shit, can't we? Play pretend a while longer? I can, anyway, even if it's starting to piss me off a little."

"It's your call."

"And so I guess we should head straight to my place and get my phone on its charger and go from there."

"You're sure that's what you want? Because I've never been rich and never planned on being rich."

"Yes, it is what I want. Especially because we can tell he still hasn't found the ticket. Or, if he did find it, it's surely not the winner."

"Right," said Adam. "And that's because . . . ?"

"Because there's no way he'd bother with me right now if he had that winning ticket in his mitts."

Adam took a good look at her. "Hmm, a night with you and Dolby or the prize of six million bucks? I know what I'd choose."

"Well, thanks, and I'd be worth every penny."

***

In his dark, cavernous living room, Mike Smith stripped to his boxers, letting his clothes fall around his feet, and then flopped back on the couch, where he grinned a very pursed grin—one of justice attained rather than delight. The hands on the clock on the wall pointed to 10:50. He turned one of the TVs to a country music station and the other to Cinemax, and then said "Like shootin' fish in a barrel!"

***

As directed by the playful Bertie and the frisky Lida, both of the Teletech stalwarts stood tall on principle and resigned by voice-message, which was a thrill for everyone involved. Bertie praised their actions as "brave and courageous," and Lida said they'd done "some pretty wild shit." She even resorted to a round of understated applause in which her palms were never more than an inch apart. Fueled by the approbation, the beer, and the prospects of a memorable night ahead, Carlos and Tyler nearly floated above their chairs. But the swell of elation got punctured the moment the check arrived. In one sense, of course, the check was welcome because until it got settled they could not leave Thirsty's and repair to a nearby apartment for some quality time with these bouncy young ladies. But, dear Jesus, the number at its bottom was offensive!

Bertie rose as she took a final swig of her final beer, and then Lida rose as well. The young women, unsteady from all the expensive ale, grabbed for their purses with both hands. Carlos and Tyler looked at each other in terror; would things come to a sudden horrible end right here? Each sought the answer in the other man's eyes, but, really, neither of them knew much about reading the opposite sex. Carlos's prior flings with women were small in number and in many ways incomplete, if not imagined; Tyler, it turns out, was even less seasoned than his bony best friend.

"Be good while we're off powdering our noses," instructed Bertie. "And keep your hands to yourselves."

"Don't do anything I wouldn't do," added Lida, proffering a wiggly fingered wave from behind her back as she too tottered off.

When the women were gone, the men breathed again. Shaking his head, Carlos said, "I should've known all along they'd do that. I mean, I've heard about how women go to the powder room together, taking their purses and everything."

"It's cool," said Tyler.

For a few minutes, the two friends were paragons of patience as they awaited the ladies' return.

"Did you see that bill?" Tyler soon asked, his own eyes double-checking it.

Carlos nodded.

"That's what? About a full day's pay? I mean, if we still had jobs. So, just how many beers did they have on us?"

"Five each."

"That's what I counted too." Tyler leaned way out to see if they were returning. "Hmm, it's taking a while. I guess all that liquid's gotta go someplace."

"Yeah, and there's probably a long line in there. Women are slow when it comes to this. There's all these layers and girdles and stuff. Plus, they have to sit down. Sitting down and then getting all the way back up, that shit takes time."

"Plus, I heard sometimes there's a couch in the ladies' johns."

Carlos gave a diagonal nod, the type that suggests conditional agreement. He said, "Yeah, I've heard that too. I don't know. I doubt they're hanging out on a couch in there. Those things are meant for women who gotta give birth all of a sudden."

***

At the southwestern tip of the county, some two miles beyond the suburban sprawl, and surrounded by prairie homes and prairies, lay a trailer park that was home to a few dozen folks and lots of dogs and cats. This particular park had been established on a modest hillside just off the two-lane highway, and now, some forty years later, the mobile homes were showing their age. From a distance they looked scattered and off-kilter, as if tossed by a tornado. In one such unit lived the notorious Lenny Buck, and that's why the gray Tempo grinded up the gravel road that same Saturday night.

Scotty said, "Remember, if Ruthie's at home we gotta be careful. Last thing she wants is somebody corrupting the man she loves."

"That woman needs to be thankful she ain't one percent uglier because then I'd go ahead and call her a man and kick her ass like a man's."

"Hey, Fobb, come on. Woman can't help it she's a mutt. You jealous that Lenny Buck found his soul mate and you're still looking?"

"Get outta here."

"Well, I'm jealous. Not ashamed to say it either. I'd sure like to be in love. You've seen the way they carry on."

"Makes me puke."

Scotty unclicked his seat belt as the car came to a stop on a weedy slope. "Me, I'm just tired of growing old all alone. No offense, Fobb, you're great and all but you ain't a lady."

"You noticed. Finally. Now hush up and let's go."

Five minutes later, inside his mobile home, the illustrious Lenny Buck said, "If I had a gun right now, I'd put a bullet in my ear. And then I'd go out and find her and put a bullet in her Goddamned ear."

"You got a hundred guns," said Scotty.

"I used to have a hundred guns. Until the yard sale."

From a couch, Fabrizio and Scotty nodded to show they cared. Across from them, in a recliner hidden in quilts, sat Lenny Buck. He was big and blunt—bigger and blunter than Mike Smith—with a face well suited for the monster movies. He now drooped that unfortunate face into both of his waiting hands.

Fabrizio said, "Hey Lenny, she'll be back. Women always come back."

"It's been almost a week. She ain't comin' back. And now I'm really in the mood to punch somebody really really hard."

***

The happy terror that Carlos and Tyler put up with for a while was now degrading into pure terror as the fellows realized the women might never return. Ten minutes had elapsed since that wiggly fingered wave that Lida proffered from behind her back.

"Did we really quit our jobs for this?" Tyler asked.

"I wish I'd called some other number and just pretended it was my manager."

"But everything happened so fast. You saw it. I mean, the beer, the smoke, the tits."

"You know anyone at work who could hack into the system and erase those messages?" asked Carlos. "Somebody on the inside maybe."

Tyler thought it over. "Drowsy Todd?"

"He can't even clean up spills. So, I don't know."

What they also didn't know was that in a dimly lit bedroom in the Deer Woods apartment complex, Bertie already lay naked under the covers with her silver-bearded husband. Less patient than the gentlemen she'd lately abandoned, she sat up and shouted, "Hurry up, baby. I'm so damn horny."

A toilet flushed. And then the red-headed Lida lumbered into view, stripping off her top as she jumped onto the bed, sending the bed, the beard, and other items bouncing.

***

Inside the mobile home, Fabrizio and Scotty made for the door with Lenny Buck right behind them. The big guy was trying to stifle his sniffling because he'd always heard rumors that tough guys never cry. The two amateur bookies helped him along by feigning sniffles themselves, as if all three men were ravaged by the September ragweed.

"Like I said, he's a brawny, dumb-looking guy," Fabrizio said. "One of them mouth-breathers, you know. Losin' his hair and all. And the stupid show-off car. You can't miss it."

"I'll find him. May take a day or two, but I'll find him. I got nothing else to do for the rest of my life, except for the funny cars which are racing next weekend out in Bonner Springs."

Scotty said, "Like we said, rough him up real good, but please don't whack him."

Opening the door, Fabrizio turned. "Yeah. A lotta ways to get your paws on what he owes us. ATM cards and plastic and all. But keep a percent for yourself."

"Save your breath. I know the ropes, Fabrizio. You think I fell off the turnip truck last week or what?"

***

By now it was late and felt even later. Adam and Lori had been squeezed for a long, long time in a car with user-unfriendly seating, and the inside of that Camry was beginning to smell like too many people. Fortunately, the car was entering the parking lot of Lori's apartment complex and they could get the hell out, stretch their legs, and inhale some fresh night air. Except, Lori was asleep.

After he parked near her building, Adam seized the opportunity to size her up. She looked very small. Her arms were bundled below her chest, and her head was bunched into the nearer corner of her back-rest, a pose that pushed her heavenly hair into a hopeless heap. Her mouth hung open like a tiny child's. Boy, she's a handful, he told himself. Now, after everything he'd been through so far that night, it was the sound of her sibilant snoring that almost made him weep.

She opened one eye. And then the other.

He cleared his throat. Tenderly, he said, "Am I gonna have to carry you in?"

Blinking away the confusion, she sat up straight and primped her hair with both hands. She looked left and then looked right and then twisted her neck in every direction to loosen it.

"Where are we?" she rasped, wiping at her mouth with the back of a hand.

"Home. Your home, I mean. I was just about to carry you in and put you into bed."

She coughed away some of the rasp, and then things went silent. It was a weird moment. They'd been through so much together, with so much still at stake, but suddenly the jackpot was the last thing on his mind because it felt like he'd reached the end of a very long, exciting, and unresolved first date—and he was a little bit nervous.

She broke the tense silence: "You don't have to carry me in, Adam. You'd probably drop me."

He forced a laugh.

A car crossed in front of them. She watched it pass. And then she looked every which way, anxiously, it seemed, and primped her hair some more. Adam wondered if she was awaiting a truly private moment so she could kiss him. Just in case, he tried to lick the dryness from his lips.

She turned and poked a finger into his tummy and murmured, "But you do need to come inside with me. And you'll find out why when we get there."

***

Among other things, Mike Smith hated proverbs because they were always kind of wimpy and boring and reminded him of four-eyed teachers and wispy hippies, and by now he hated the proverb "patience is a virtue" more than any other proverb in the world. To his view, patience was for losers because the patient were unable or unwilling to exert their power to conquer external factors and submit those factors to their own preferred schedule—that is, if one were to put words into his mouth. Now, impatient, alone, and hung out to dry in his burgundy boxers and gym socks, he tramped from window to door to window, cursing that stuck-up, blonde-ass bitch with all his power and fury.

***

Inside her apartment, Lori flicked the nearest light switch and continued to the kitchen, where she deposited her purse and her phone on the island.

"I'm so thirsty," she moaned. "It feels like they're manufacturing peanut butter in my mouth. Beer or soda pop?"

"Beer, if you are," he creaked, his mouth dusty as well.

"Hungry?"

"Naah. Too worked up. I'm way past an appetite right now."

"Same here." She got out two bottles of a local brew and then stood beside Adam in the center of her kitchen, where together they guzzled. Soon she stifled the smallest of belches, wiped her mouth with her hand, and began the explanation she'd earlier teased:

"So, I've got it figured out. And it's gonna sound counter-intuitive. But bear with me. We should not call the brute right now. It could ruin everything."

Tenderly, he said, "Hey, I get it. That's fine by me."

She stepped forward until they were across from each other. "No, I'm not afraid of him. What I'm gonna suggest is logical; it has nothing to do with him being a shithead. All right? So, look, I know we've been focusing on where he lives. But right now what really matters is he knows where I live. So, I think we'd agree for the past half-hour he's been waiting for me, buck naked except for brown socks, and he's as mad as a hornet by now."

"Oh I'm sure he's been bonered up for a long time."

"Yes, and he has a massive ego. He's a narcissist, right? And narcissists have little control over their impulses. So any minute now he'll be on his way over here to really let me have it. I mean, what's to stop him?"

"Nothing, I guess."

"You're exactly right," she said, tapping his bicep with the base of her beer bottle. "Nothing. Except for a phone call from me. Because then he could just batter me over the phone, which might defuse his anger just enough—just enough—to keep him from driving over here."

"Okay, but we've agreed the man is very horned up, so maybe he wouldn't go ballistic on you in the first place and risk losing that chance for the . . . good thing."

"Hey, I promise you anger trumps lust every time for these spoiled brats. You've heard what the experts say about rape?"

"It's an act of violence," he answered, nodding.

"Violence. Power. Control. And anger, of course. This Mike Smith, I don't think he's a rapist, per se, but he's definitely abusive and has to have power and control."

"Wait. So hang on. Let me summarize all of this, just to make sure." He lowered his beer and backed against the refrigerator. "If you were to call him and just ask for his address like we planned, that would be a bad idea. Right?"

"Yes, because we don't want to give him any opportunity to defuse his wrath. Okay? We want him to stay completely mad because—and this is what matters the most—we actually want him to come here."

"And remind me why. God, it's late. It's been a very long day and we're gettin' too old for this shit."

Grinning, she put the bottle on the countertop behind her so she could use both hands to illustrate her words. "Okay. One, a little while ago we concluded he hasn't found the ticket. Remember?"

Adam nodded. "He'd have better fish to fry than bothering to mess with us, yes."

"Right. So that makes it more likely the bag and thus the ticket are still in the car. Not a sure thing, but we have to play the odds, like you always say. Two, in one minute we will therefore get on our knees and patrol from a window in there, in my living room, and watch for the Porsche. When we see it pull up, you'll step out to the balcony and hop down to the grass and sneak out to the parking lot."

"Jump down? How high are we?"

"It's not much. I've done it a few times myself."

"No lie? How come?"

"To show off. Okay, so step three, once he's up here banging on my door, you'll be able to peep into his car window and look for the bag. If it's in there, then that information will be helpful at least."

"It would be nice to know," he said.

"Now, you wanna hear my best-case scenario? Because I'm thinking—hoping—he could be so mad, so worked up, so in a froth that he forgets to lock the car. I'd say there's a thirty percent chance you could just reach in and take your jeans if the bag's still there."

"God, that would be perfect."

"Wouldn't it?" she said with a wonderful grin.

"But there's so many ifs."

"True, but it's probably the best plan we've got. Look, if he does lock the car, then how might you feel about following him home after he gives up here? That way, we'd at least know where he lives, and maybe we could use that info later. Pull some kind of ruse or something. Cable repairman or . . . or traveling tailors . . . or whatnot?"

"Sure. I don't mind tracking him home. It might be fun."

Lori exhaled mightily and then made for the kitchen island. She asked him to fetch a couple more beers while she finally placed her phone on its charger.

***

If only Lori had put the phone on the charger one minute earlier, things might have transpired much differently, for better or worse. That's because the moment she was asking Adam Durham to get two more bottles of beer, Mike Smith's fingers were pressing her phone number. And because Lori Nelson's phone was completely, defiantly without battery power and not yet connected to the charger, the call went straight to voice mail, which inspired him to heave his phone into the couch and then to clutch for the clothes still strewn on the carpet.

***

Adam volunteered for the first patrol shift. He dimmed the lighting in the living room and knelt at the east window, where he sipped his second beer and shook his head a lot as he pondered everything in a desperately shallow fashion, as if he were flipping among news channels that were devoted to his night alone. Soon the pilsner relaxed him, and so he closed his eyes, just for a moment. But a commotion nearby opened his eyes. Lori, now in summer shorts and a sleeveless tee, had dropped to her knees beside him. Her bare shins brushed against his bare shins, which sent a million pins prickling from his head to his toes.

"I'm both wide awake and exhausted," she grieved, leaning forward and resting her chin on the sill, which was not a comfortable pose at all. She raised the chin. "I hate that combination. Amped up and worn out at the same time. Electric eyes. Heavy eyes. I just wanna sleep but I'm sure I can't, and I don't think I should."

"You?" he said, surprised. "You don't strike me as someone who ever has trouble sleeping. Did I tell you about my roommate from Joplin? I bet you he's into his second or third hour of peaceful sleep by now."

"Him again."

"The man haunts me, Lori."

"Well, might I suggest you get over it? And might I also suggest you go spread out on the couch and relax. I can take it from here. Actually, I'm beginning to worry he won't come by after all. That I was wrong about the whole thing. I'd say if he's not pounding on that door within five minutes, then we can probably call it a night."

"The bastard's probably snoring away by now, like my old roommate. I bet this Mike Smith's the type of guy who never has a problem sleeping."

"Go lay down, Adam. Please. Go rest your eyes and your brain, as it were. I can manage this for a while."

"It might feel good to spread out for a bit," he conceded, rising from his knees. "But I won't sleep. Not a chance. I'm way too jazzed up for that."

Five minutes later, sprawled and flat on that couch like a chalked-out homicide victim, Adam was snoring with impressive consistency. Nearby, Lori lay crumpled at the window in a sleep so deep that she did not hear the snoring or the sound of her phone chirping from its charger on the kitchen island. And, for the record, she didn't hear the ceaseless honking that originated from Mike Smith's Porsche 911. But to hear the honking would have been miraculous because Mike Smith was honking that horn in the parking lot of the Deer Creek apartments, a mile or so away.

Sunday the 21st

Four hours passed before Adam opened an eye and saw the lovely face of Lori Nelson one foot away from that eye. She was on her knees beside the couch. Her hair was wet and falling; she leaned so close that its damp tips stung his cheeks like icicles.

In a whisper, she said, "Guess what I realized a few minutes ago. Brody's has to have a security camera."

He squeezed shut that burning eye. His dinger, too, was burning with the profound desire to pee.

"Adam, don't you understand what this means? If they have tape of you buying that ticket at the right moment, it might be enough to take to court, if Mike Smith tries to cash in."

Adam willed open both of his eyes. "What time is it?"

"Three-fifty."

"Well, I better get up. I've got that paper route."

She leaned back and rested on her haunches. "Sorry. I got excited and couldn't sleep."

"Do I smell as bad as I feel?"

"You must feel rotten. You can take a shower if you want."

"Camera, huh?"

"Why not? I mean, we've hassled a cop, we've put a thousand miles on your car, I've left raunchy phone messages—"

"No, you might be on to something." He sat up and held his chin.

Lori went to the kitchen and got out her phone book. "I'm calling Brody's, just to make sure they have that tape. I'll feel a whole lot better if they do. They're open around the clock, aren't they?"

He reached for his shoes. "Don't say a word about the ticket. We don't need any more complications."

"Don't worry. I gave it a lot of thought in the shower. I've got a plan."

After a most pleasing piss, Adam entered the kitchen in time to observe the call, which Lori made with her fully charged phone. In this instance, she claimed to be an Officer Miller with the Southland precinct. Soon she said, "No, sir. Nobody ratted on you. We're not interested in you. Listen, we believe a convicted drug dealer was in your store Friday, just after noon, actually." She listened for a moment. Then: "Yes, twelve noon." She winked at Adam. Then: "No, it doesn't matter that you weren't there. We just need to know how long you keep the recordings from your security cameras." Again, she listened. "Oh, you're sure of that? Because you can get in trouble for lying to an officer of the law." Lori was silent for ten seconds, and then her brows arched and she seemed to lean into the phone call: "What do you mean suspicious? He's doing what? With his . . . ? That is weird. You better hang up and call the cops right now!"

Near the door, Adam waited with keys in hand.

Lori put the phone down and folded her arms. "Just our luck. Their camera's been on the fritz for a month."

"It figures. Their Slurpee machine never works either."

She dropped into a kitchen chair and folded her arms crisply.

"I'll be in touch before noon," he said, jingling his keys. "Maybe we'll figure something out if it's not too late."

"Yeah, go get some real rest. Maybe without me around you'll be able to think clearly."

"Same to you. I mean, I've always thought 'team-think' was over-rated. The dynamic of it all, you know. Not wanting to hurt anyone's feelings, and seeking approval, and actually being insecure about your own – wait!" He pointed past her. "Your phone's blinking. Didn't you notice?"

She turned in her chair. Reaching, she said, "Oh my God. How'd I miss it? I hate this new phone." She looked closely at it and then rose and put the device to her ear. Adam came nearer, but she turned her back as she listened to the message Mike Smith had left some hours ago while honking like mad in the wrong parking lot. Then she snapped the phone shut and slid it across the kitchen table as if it were radioactive.

"What?" he whispered.

"Nothing." She folded her arms and walked around the island, head down.

"You okay?"

"No one's ever spoken to me like that. And I thought I was prepared for it."

"Hey, I'm sorry. Look, I don't know what he said, but whatever the bastard said, I know the exact opposite is true."

Although tears slid down her cheeks, Lori's composure remained intact and her voice unbroken. "No big surprise, Adam. Pretty predictable. He said I was a whore. And I'm starting to wonder if he's right. Talking to him like I did."

He shoved his car keys into his pocket and came two steps closer, his eyes tearing as well. "Lori, you're so far from being that. It's all my fault, dragging you into this stupid thing. I'm so sorry."

She forced a smile as Adam reached for a paper towel. She took it, crumpled it, and dabbed her eyes. "You didn't drag me into anything. I barged in."

"No—"

"It's okay. I'm okay. His opinion means nothing to me. I swear it. It's just that I'm so tired and everything, and so disappointed we haven't figured all this out. And . . . that I'm letting you down and everything."

"What? No way!" He squeezed out the flattest of chuckles and then said, "You aren't letting me down 'cuz I never thought you were all that clever in the first place."

She pushed out an equally flat smile and flatly said, "Thanks, thanks. That's super news. Oh, Adam, man, this night has worn me down. This whole thing's put us through the wringer. I've never been through anything like this."

"Well I hope not."

Lori laughed and slapped her head. "Of course. Duh." She gestured with her right hand, her fingers waving to the kitchen floor as if urging a house pet along: "Go rest a while. Please. We can fight the good fight later today."

"You sure I should go?"

She nodded.

"Call me if you need to. Because even though you're a pain in the ass, I for one will answer."

***

Because of their misfortunes at Thirsty Mack's, Carlos Williams and Tyler Jones hadn't slept well either. The prospects of six million dollars were not on their minds, but plenty of other things were. Carlos, in particular, kept reminding himself to view the events in total as instructional: Those who fail to learn from history are doomed to repeat their mistakes, he twice told himself. The problem was, he didn't exactly know what the lesson was. But he feared the lesson was this: Be handsome and charming and possibly rich. At any rate, by ten a.m. he was at his computer, browsing the website Monster.com. There were dozens of openings in town, but he wasn't sure how to pare them to a realistic few since he wasn't sure what he did at Teletech.

In his own apartment, his chubby friend, Tyler, soaked in a bath as he scanned the classified ads in the Sunday paper. He too had suffered a mostly sleepless night. Much to his surprise, he'd fallen asleep quickly, owing to sheer exhaustion, but ten minutes into his slumber he was rudely awakened by some idiot in the parking lot who leaned on his car horn for the longest time. Tyler had clambered out of bed to get a good look at the type of idiot who would lean on a car horn for such a long time after midnight. And, of course, the guy was a rich guy in a sports car. Probably a handsome guy, too. Tyler halfway wished he was the type of guy who could get away with blasting a horn in the middle of the night like that. The whole thing angered him so much that he fidgeted and fretted in bed for a few more hours.

***

As noon neared, Lori and Adam ate sandwiches and apple slices in her tidy kitchen and made the smallest of small talk. After a bit of silence, they locked eyes, until she chuckled.

"What now?"

"Hey Adam. You stink at all this."

"At all what?"

"This sleuthing. The whole thing."

He pointed hard at her. "So do you! Yes, you. A project manager, for God's sake."

"Maybe I do."

"And you love this stuff. You live for it all. Planning and strategizing, putting together tables and diagrams, and making all the right faces during those stupid meetings and using all the right buzzwords. You're supposed to be good at it."

"What I do at work is called play-acting. I put on costumes five days a week and play-act, and I happen to be pretty good at it, and maybe sometimes I even enjoy the whole thing. I mean, why not at least try to enjoy it somehow?"

"So that's your story now?" he asked dubiously, his head aslant. "Sounds like I've gotten to ya. Because last night you said you'd keep your job if you got the millions."

"I never said that. What I implied was I'd do something. Certainly not Teletech, if that makes you happy. I mean, come on. That heartless place? But yes, I'd do something useful with my time or else I might end up like one of those old ladies who . . . collects hairpins in coffee cans." She pushed her plate away. "But, listen, while we're on the topic, how'd you like some cheap advice?"

He backed away in his chair. "The last time I took some cheap advice, I bought a lottery ticket."

"Ah. I will happily avoid that line of questioning. Anyway, here's my cheap advice: don't quit your day job to become a detective."

He slapped the table as if in triumph. "Too late. I already quit."

"What?"

"Months ago. I just haven't told anyone yet."

"Well . . . then good. Yes. You should leave that place. Tomorrow. Tomorrow you need to tell someone."

"I think I'll do that."

"And then go find out what color your parachute is, whatever that means."

"I can figure that out later, if I need to. I mean, three million can delay a lot of harsh choices."

While Adam cleared the table, Lori pulled open the dishwasher. With her head halfway inside the appliance, she returned to the topic they'd been skirting ever since Adam's return: she needed to call Mike Smith again.

"No, I think I should call him. You've taken enough abuse."

"You honestly want to?" she asked.

He nodded.

"What's your plan?"

"I don't know. I'm tempted to wing it. That's how I've gotten through life so far."

"That explains a lot," she said.

"Well, I don't think our original plan would still make sense, after you stiffing him last night? He wouldn't fall for your teasing and flirting one more time, would he?"

She shook her head as she gave him the phone. "Yeah, we've burned that bridge. Though, I can't believe he never showed up last night. Hmm, maybe I don't have everything figured out after all. Well . . . so maybe it is time we just play it straight up. No more drama. No more scheming. Look, if he answers, don't mention the ticket, of course, but just ask him for your jeans back and we'll see what happens. Something will happen. And at this point, that's better than nothing."

***

At Jiffy Jeff's Car Wash in southern Johnson County, the youthful crew worked hard to make every customer's vehicle sparkle inside and out. In the case of a certain Porsche 911, the cleaning regimen included folding a pair of blue jeans that were found bunched on the rear floorboard and placing them on the rear passenger seat. Charlie, an assistant manager, next drove the sports car to the waiting area for disposition to its owner. He exited the car, whistled, and pointed to Mike Smith, who was sitting in a patio chair nearby while the world played out in reverse upon his elite shades.

"Nice ride," called Charlie as the burly customer passed him.

"I hear yuh."

Just as the car's rightful owner climbed inside, his phone signaled. He shut the door, checked the caller ID, and then eagerly answered the dispatch with these words: "Lady, you really do have a low opinion of yourself."

But the caller's voice surprised him almost as much as the words it spoke. "Hey man, listen, through a strange deal my jeans ended up in your gym bag the other night at that pool party."

"Who's this? Where's the girl?"

Lori waved at Adam and whispered, "Just the jeans. The jeans."

"Yeah, I'd like to go ahead and get those jeans back, man."

"Hey, I remember you. The guy in the trunks. So what are you doing with her phone?"

"So, like, can I just whiz on by and get my jeans real quick?"

Mike Smith lifted his sunglasses and gave the car's interior a quick glance. The gym bag was not there, of course—he remembered having struggled to free it the other night—but he did spot the folded jeans, practically gift wrapped on that back seat, placed there by a Jiffy Jeff associate, no doubt. The whole thing made him laugh. He said, "Uhm, the jeans? The jeans? Let me tell you what I did with those jeans, friend. Used 'em to wipe my poodle's ass." And for his own amusement he made a production of snapping the phone shut.

***

No one in particular was watching Mike Smith savor his small moment of triumph, but someone was certainly looking for him. Not far away, an old Chevy pickup truck, one that would have profited from a visit to Jiffy Jeff's Car Wash, rumbled down a crowded four-lane avenue. The driver of the yellow truck wore a menacing expression; he'd been on the hunt for a couple hours so far, and it appeared the menacing expression had gotten stuck on his face, a consequence many parents had warned their kids about since time immemorial.

***

Adam plunked his forehead onto Lori's kitchen table. "I should've let you handle it."

"I'd have never taken him for a poodle owner," she said.

"I should've let you handle it," he repeated.

She rose because she could no longer sit still. "Oh Adam, I think we got too impatient. Both of us. Thinking he'd ever be reasonable."

"We had to try something. I mean, I'm sure there are elaborate ploys out there we'll think of later today or twenty years from now, but . . . ."

"I know. That's gonna sting. The obvious path is out there somewhere. But for now I just hope to death he doesn't find that ticket. I don't think I could live with that. But it'd take a real miracle for him not to find it now."

Adam lifted his head. "But he still hadn't found it. He still knew nothing about it. Otherwise he'd be gloating like crazy."

"True, but right now I bet he's digging your jeans from that stupid gym bag and rifling the pockets. And the jig will be up. What do you say we go kill ourselves together?"

***

In a corner of a mall parking lot stood an olive-green trailer with a large, handwritten sign that said "We buy Jean's!" Near the trailer in a canvas chair sat Viktor, an Eastern European man of sixty. He was rotund, bald on top, and silvery around the ears. The structure of his jowls and chin was identical to that of the American comedian Don Rickles, but he was heavy lidded and wore a drowsy expression. Viktor was reading a magazine, his bare feet crossed on a card table, when a Porsche 911 stopped much too close to him. Its driver, Mike Smith, was a man in a hurry. Dangling on one arm was a pair of blue jeans. Its front pockets dangled as well, rabbit-eared, white upon denim blue.

"What'll these bring?" he demanded, still irked that those two pockets had been empty.

A former member of the Soviet secret police, Viktor was indifferent to any belligerent tone, especially one purveyed by a pasty, middle-aged middle American in a polo shirt and Topsiders, and so he accepted the jeans at his customary leisurely pace. He gave the garment the quickest of looks before tossing it upon the table. "Five bucks."

Mike jabbed a finger towards Viktor's paunch. "Got yourself a deal."

Viktor told him to toss the jeans into the trailer, and then he leaned and fished a five-spot from his money belt and held it out, folded between his fingers.

Mike Smith took the bill and glanced at a young woman that queued behind him, each arm holding department-store bags that were bulging with blue jeans. On either side of the woman were excitable kids, creeping and oozing and slinking all over, seeming to multiply before his eyes like bacteria. He turned back to Viktor. "Got some more jeans at home that are too tight in the crouch. How long you here?"

"Truck picks up the trailer in forty-five minutes."

"Hmm. Probably take me an hour. Can they hold it for me?"

"No can do," said Viktor, looking down into his magazine again.

"You serious?"

"No can do."

"That sucks."

Mike Smith intended to return home and get those spare jeans and bring them to the trailer anyway, because that's the way he did business, but on the way out he was seduced by the powerful aroma of deep-fried chicken. He veered left and angled the Porsche into the parking lot of Chicken Marvin's, where that fresh five-dollar bill would come in handy.

***

Two blocks to the west of there, just beyond the influence of Chicken Marvin's aromatic plume, Lenny Buck was as wide-eyed as ever in his yellow pick-up truck. For the first time since Ruthie left him, he was feeling like his old good self, and it was all because of this most impossible assignment: to find a single sports car in a vast and dense county. The whole thing made Lenny Buck feel alive again, re-animated, as it were. In fact, the hours of surveilling felt like minutes to him! Cruising along, the big, big man happily punched the steering wheel and chanted this eerie mantra: "Red Porsche. Red Porsche. Red Porsche."

***

Despite its appetizing aroma, the food at Chicken Marvin's was unexceptional. But Mike Smith knew the place was trendy, almost as trendy as The Remarkable Rib, which happened to be owned by the same conglomerate from Salt Lake City, and if a place was trendy, that meant it was good enough for Mike Smith. Chicken Marvin's had gotten its cachet from being featured on a Food Network program called "Culinary Cut-Ups," which liked the way the restaurant greeted its customers. To wit, any time a guest entered, the front crew would sing out this delightful refrain: "Step right up; hope you're starvin' / Can't go wrong at Chicken Marvin's."

So, naturally, when Mike Smith entered, he was greeted with the catchy couplet. It was, if you put two and two together, the reason he was there, but still he sneered at the gimmick and pushed out his palms in an effort to keep those minimum-wage losers at bay while he scanned the big-board menu.

***

Tyler Jones knelt at his toilet while his finger poked out the work number of his former supervisor. He sensed it would be safest to explain things by voice mail in order to prevent any conversational give and take, whereby he'd just make matters worse. Plus, if he should happen to vomit in mid-sentence, he could choose to delete the message and start over.

In his most polite tone, he said, "Hey, Sherry. Hi! This is Tyler Jones. Hey, you may have gotten, like, a strange voice mail from me kind of late on Saturday night and stuff. I'd like to, uhm, apologize for that and also for the stuff I said about the Teletech board and their fringe benefits and all. And quitting. I didn't really mean to quit or anything. Plus, I'd also like to go ahead and make it clear that I'd been drinking heavily, which is not something I often do." In a whisper, he soon added this: "A girl made me do it."

Carlos Williams, meanwhile, was browsing balloon bouquets in a gift shop and silently forming the phrasing he'd use when he made his own phone call to his own former supervisor's voice machine in a little while.

***

Meanwhile, Adam and Lori were again at her kitchen table, suppressing a sense of doom as they reviewed a bulleted list of schemes and tactics they'd already exhausted. Frankly, the two had no new plans in mind and figured at this point it would be futile to get back into a car and prowl. What really mattered was this: Mike Smith knew about the jeans for sure, and it was likely he'd scavenged the pockets and found the ticket.

"That ticket better be a loser," Lori growled, "or I'll be in a bad mood for the rest of my life."

"He doesn't deserve such joy. I mean, to that guy, winning six million would be, like, the highlight of his life because he's such a materialist. But with us, it'd only be a nice to have, am I right?"

Lori nodded and then pushed the legal pad with such force that it fell off the table.

"Except, maybe there is a slender bit of hope," Adam claimed. "The ticket is pretty thin and wispy after all, and I did stick it in a back pocket, so maybe it got past him."

"The eternal optimist over here," she muttered to unseen friends, pointing at him with a thumb.

"If you just pat down the back pocket, you wouldn't notice it, I bet."

And then her phone cheeped.

"Oh my God," she said, seeing the caller's name. "This can't be good."

"You talk. Please. I've done enough damage by now."

She stood and achieved some distance from the chirping item, as if it was an asp in mid coil. "He's calling to gloat. He's got the winning ticket. Why else would he call? Oh man, this will certainly be the worst minute of my life." She lunged for the device.

From a primo booth inside Chicken Marvin's, Mike Smith spoke. "Ah,

Lori. Breaking news."

She held strong against his gleeful tone and did her best to sound bored. "What?"

"Tell your new boyfriend—so is he your boyfriend?"

"What's it to you?"

"Anyway, tell that guy he'll never see his crappy jeans again. Hope they meant a lot to him."

She waited an extra second. "So . . . is that all?" Her final syllables lilted because he hadn't mentioned the ticket!

"Well, what more do you—"

"That's just weak, Mike Smith. Your life must be pretty hollow if you go out of your way to call us about a silly pair of jeans. That's thin soup, I have to say, Mike Smith. Thin soup."

"Hey, you suck. I mean, one minute you're calling to fuck me and the next you—"

Grinning helplessly, Lori lowered the phone because it sounded like he was starting another rant. More than that, she wanted to put the phone back on the table so she could throw both arms in the air in relief! But when Adam saw the device at her thigh, he assumed the conversation was over and the call disconnected. He came closer and rejoiced: "Someone ain't found the ticket yet!"

Lori's face got all twisted and white like an unbaked pretzel as she slapped a hand over the phone. "He's still there," she hissed, bending her whole body.

Adam responded with the default "I messed up" expression: wide eyes, high brows, distorted lower lip.

She put the phone to her ear again just in time to hear Mike Smith say "Ticket?"

"No," she said.

"I heard ticket."

"Nobody said ticket."

"So that's what it's all about in the first place. A-ha. There's a ticket in them jeans. Wait, are you sure? Because . . . unless it's in a back pocket because . . . ." He then chortled. "All these calls and stuff, I guess that ticket must be pretty valuable."

"Uh, there's no ticket," she said feebly.

"Bet it's for Faith Hill. Yep. That concert's already sold out. Is that it? She's smokin' hot. I bet you wish you were as hot as her."

"I do. So where are the jeans?"

"Like I'd tell you. Because, you see, that ticket is not your business anymore. That ticket's mine."

Adam was doing his best to draw logical conclusions from hearing one side of the dialog, but now, impulsively, and without Lori's permission, he stepped closer and leaned toward the phone and said, "I can prove I bought it when the winner was sold at Brody's!"

Lori couldn't pull the device away in time to prevent most of Adam's message from being conveyed. Shaking her head, she gave the phone to him, whispering "I give up. You're so impulsive."

"What?" he said innocently as he took the phone. Adam looked at her for two seconds, his mouth open, before placing the device at his ear. Then, dejectedly, he spoke into it: "Hey."

The reality of the millions must have sunk into Mike Smith's head because his phone voice was now less obnoxious: "So, even better. A lottery ticket? I saw the news on that. The winning lottery ticket's in those jeans?"

Adam was surprised to hear such a civil tone. Hell, maybe they could work something out after all. There really was plenty of money to go around. Why not peacefully co-exist? Why not be grown-ups? He arched a brow at Lori and said to Mike Smith, "It might be the winner. Might be. Hey, all I know is I bought it at the right time and the right place. So let's be reasonable here. We can all come out okay on this. Six million can go pretty far, you know."

"You mean, you bought it at the right Brody's and all?"

"Yes. It all matches. Time and place, I mean. But I never looked at the numbers so I don't know."

"Did you sign it?"

"Uh, of course."

The civil tone vanished. "I don't believe you. And anyways, I can see for myself."

"Then tell me what the numbers are."

"Forget you."

"Why not?" snapped Adam.

"Because it's not in my hands at the moment."

"I can wait."

"Kiss my balls," he said, a bit too loudly in such a public spot.

"Do you even have my jeans?"

"Why wouldn't I?"

"Then go check the ticket numbers. That'll answer everything right now. I'll wait."

"You're not my boss."

The fact that Mike Smith was paying attention to him instead of exiting the phone call, fetching the jeans, and checking the numbers was a clue that gave Adam another glimmer of hope. He said, "It appears to me you don't have the jeans, unless you're just enjoying this conversation so much. Ha! You must've thrown 'em out already. Ha! That's it!"

"Nope."

Grinning, he winked at Lori. "And some of these new neighborhoods have their trash pickups on Saturdays. I know because a guy at work was griping about how the trucks wake him up when he's hung over. Yes, that's it! You live in one of those neighborhoods, and so those jeans are in the dump right now. So nobody wins! I can live with that."

Lori lowered her head, made a fist, and threw that fist.

"No, butt-munch. I know exactly where they are and you don't. Swear to God, man. That's the truth."

"Then where are they?" Adam made a very hard swallow.

"Right. Like I'm gonna tell you. Hey, listen, in a couple minutes they'll be back in my hands and the jackpot's gonna be mine."

"Why should I believe you?"

"Because you should."

"Wait! In case you're telling the truth, I've got the law on my side. I've got witnesses. There's a yogurt thing in my car trash, for God's sake! Look, we can make this work. Keep it out of the courts. How about . . . how about you just safeguard that ticket and . . . and twenty percent is yours." Adam looked at Lori. She nodded and stuck a finger down her throat.

"How generous," said Mike Smith from that booth at Chicken Marvin's. "Twenty percent. But I'd prefer to negotiate with the lady of the house."

"Why? I mean, the amount is—"

"The lady!"

Adam lowered the phone and looked at Lori.

"What?" she said sternly.

Adam put his hand over it. "He swears he can get the jeans back, whatever that means. I don't know. They're probably in his trash or something. And he wants to bargain with you. Are you up to it?"

"Gimme that." She grabbed the phone. "What?"

Mike Smith greeted her with more invective, and then he spoke slowly, just to savor each syllable and rub it all in. "Okay, here's the bargain: I get a hundred percent of the jackpot and you two losers get zilch. How do you like them apples?"

Her grin got larger than her face. "Mike Smith, it's a deal!" She squeezed shut the phone and grabbed her purse and charged for the door. "Come on, Adam. Fast! It's all goin' down, so get out your keys and run like the wind!"

***

Mike Smith had every reason to be baffled by Lori's reaction. He even spent a moment staring into his device for answers, as if cell-phone technology really could provide an actual solution to something in life that mattered. Did that broad really agree to such a bad deal? Of course she did. Probably because he was, after all, Mike Smith.

He rose from the booth, wiped some crumbs from his shirt, and made for the exit. He had enough time to get those jeans back from the trailer before the big truck would arrive, assuming the truck wasn't early. And then, Jesus Christ, he'd have a passport to real wealth. But halfway to the door, he stopped. He took another step forward and stopped once more. He held that spot for a moment. Then, finally, he proceeded straight out the door and into the sunlight. He could see the jeans trailer up the hill, close but too far to walk. He could even make out Viktor's shoes crossed upon the table. But just before he could open his car door, Mike Smith clutched his gut, clenched his butt cheeks, and hurried back inside the restaurant, where he was promptly greeted with a familiar refrain: "Step right up; hope you're starvin' / Can't go wrong at Chicken Marvin's."

***

In the Deer Run parking lot, Adam gassed the Camry toward an exit as Lori clued him in: "He's at that Chicken Marvin's up on Antioch. I heard those workers in the background. You know, they yell that corny rhyme all the time? We can be there in five minutes if we make the lights."

"Excellent! Excellent! And then what?"

"And then we follow him home."

"Excellent! And then what?"

"And then . . . together we kick his ass and get what's rightfully ours."

"God, you're gonna get us killed, but you are fun!"

***

In the men's room, Mike Smith sat upon one of Chicken Marvin's two toilets. He was made so furious by this untimely call from nature that none of the comical graffiti around him raised the slightest of smiles. Of course he'd tried to will away the urgings while outside, but it felt like a dozen dwarves were tugging at his waistline while a dozen midgets were punching him just the same. The moment his intestines had begun bubbling, blurping, and gurgling like an aquarium, he knew it was time to surrender. Yes, Mike Smith had lost a battle, but it was only a battle. Still, if he didn't speed things along he might lose a big, big war because that big truck from Russia would arrive in minutes to take away his big lottery ticket, worth six million dollars.

He looked at his watch. This was going to be close.

***

Adam gunned it through a yellow light, took the next turn, and then bounded into a strip mall parking lot. It was Lori who spotted the Porsche.

"It looks empty. He must still be inside the place," she said, pointing at the car.

Adam pulled next to the Porsche, but before the car stopped, Lori was halfway out its door. She cupped her hands at the Porsche's windows and then turned and shook her head. "No jeans. No bag."

But she did spot something in the distance. She took one step past the Camry, paused, and took another and another. Adam opened his door and leaned on it.

"You see it?" she called, still sidling away.

He looked to the southwest and saw it.

"Let's go!" she exclaimed.

"Wait! If we're wrong, he'll come out and drive off and then we've lost him. Which is a very big deal if those jeans are still in his house."

"I bet they're up there. But . . . okay, there's no harm in penning him in, I guess. Can you back out and then pull in so tight he cannot get in that door? But hurry, man! He's gonna notice us."

"Can't he just use the passenger door?"

"Adam, he's a big guy and it's a tiny car and he's not very bright. It'll take him forever to figure it out, and he'll stand there cussing awhile, and then it'll take him forever to actually climb across. This'll buy us time in case you're right and the jeans are not up there. It's all we can do."

And so he put the Camry in reverse.

One minute later, as they approached the trailer, the couple slowed to a brisk walk. Adam looked over his shoulder and said, "Damn, the smart thing would've been for one of us to stay back at the car. In case he drives off and all."

"Damn, I hate it when you're right. But we're here now."

"Okay, use your charm on this guy."

"Charm, hell. I'm relying on cash."

Viktor's nose peeked over his magazine as they neared.

"Hey, did a big guy in a Porsche sell a pair of jeans today?"

"Huh? About thirty, forty minutes ago," he said, sizing her up and down.

"Yes!" exclaimed Adam, making a fist.

Grinning, Lori reached into her pocket and pulled out a twenty and a ten. "We want to buy 'em back."

"Heh-heh, I'd be a fool to refuse a profit like that." He took the cash and pointed at the trailer behind him.

"They'll be easy to find?"

"I bought twenty-six pairs right after that guy was here. And the lady paid me ten bucks to let her grimy kids play in there so she could have a smoke in peace. Sounded like a madhouse. Kids love to play with the blue jeans, you know."

They looked into the trailer, which was teeming with enough denims to clothe every asshole in the county.

"Plus, looks like you got maybe seven minutes before the truck gets here to take 'em away. That sum-bitch is always on time. That's how they do it in Russia. Or else they get executed."

Adam and Lori climbed inside it, no further questions asked.

"What's our system?"

"Just grab," he said. "It's all we have time for. And check the back pockets. Left side only."

Owing to the kids' fervor, many of the jeans in that unit were entangled like snakes that had gone through the laundry together. The couple uncoiled, tugged, inspected, and tossed with such haste that sometimes multiple pairs were aloft at once. Meanwhile, Viktor leaned his elbows on his table, chewed nicotine gum, and continued to read his magazine.

***

To their north, Mike Smith was zipping up even as he neared his car. "What the fuck?" he said aloud, seeing the Camry so close to his car. He turned all the way around and asked a phantom audience "How'm I supposed to get in?" He pounded his forearm on the hood of that Toyota only one time because he was in a rush. He then unlocked his passenger door and clambered inside and into the driver's seat with surprising facility.

***

A hundred yards to his east, the gruesome driver of a yellow pickup truck was waiting a lifetime to turn into that same parking lot. He'd already spotted the cherry-red Porsche with pinstripes – the sight of it made him exclaim "Jackpot!" But it would take the damn traffic light at least a couple minutes to cycle through.

***

Adam and Lori continued scrapping and scrambling inside that hot trailer, the cracks of their asses exposed. Even through the echoes of their grunts and gasps, they heard Viktor say "You again."

The tone of his voice stopped them both. They crawled northward and popped their heads into the sunlight, spotting the Porsche. They next saw Mike Smith. And Mike Smith saw them. He stopped. He pointed. He advanced.

"Those are my jeans they're trying to steal!"

"No they're not!" Lori shouted.

Sounding bored, Viktor said, "Lady's right. I gave you five bucks for 'em. So why not do me a favor and get lost?"

Mike Smith's response was a pitiful mixture of threats, oaths, and pleas, so dull that Adam and Lori went back to work, and in seconds Adam found a pair of jeans that somehow in that sea of jeans looked familiar. He slipped his left hand into the left-side back pocket. He grinned. He raised the garment high.

"Yes!" he exclaimed in a sibilant whisper that resonated throughout the canister, as if there were indeed dozens of hissing entangled snakes inside it. Seeing his grin first and the jeans second, Lori tossed the trousers that were in her own two hands. In synch, the young couple flopped backwards onto the choppy sea of dungarees and lay there kicking their legs in the air and cackling like demons.

Mike Smith burled past Viktor's table and bellied up to the mouth of the trailer, demanding to know if they'd found the winner.

Lori got on her knees and ordered him back with her words and the thrust of an arm. Adam rose to his knees as well and answered the question: "Lori and I are gonna find out together."

"Don't look at it! Don't! I'll buy that ticket. I swear I'll buy it, sight unseen."

Adam clutched the jeans to his chest. "Hey, now back up. Back up. Let's all be cool here. Let's be civilized."

Surprisingly, Mike Smith retreated in small steps as Adam dropped outside to the pavement. He put his hand in the back pocket of those jeans as if clutching a grenade. Lori jumped down beside him.

"I can feel it," he said to Lori. "It's still there! Man, this ticket! What a trooper!"

"Sight unseen, bro. Fifty grand." Mike Smith's body language was like that of an FBI negotiator dealing with an armed madman. Pointing, he said, "See that bank? And there's one behind the Yarn Barn and another one over by the Lofty Headware. I got accounts at all three."

"They're closed," said Lori.

"ATMs never close. Listen, I can grab four grand from each one. No lie. Plus fifteen grand in cash advances on my plastic. Right now. No lie. I'm a platinum member. No lie. Write you a check for the rest. On the spot. Serious as a heart attack."

Once again Adam looked at Lori. "Fifty grand?"

She said, "It's your ticket."

"It's our ticket."

"You should decide. You're the one who bought it."

"But you've paid the price."

Nearby, Viktor rolled his eyes as he turned the magazine page.

Mike Smith stamped a foot. Squinting, he shielded his eyes with his flattened hand and said, "Look, you said yourself it might not be the winner. So I'm the one takin' a gamble here." He stared hard at Adam, his cheeks darkening in the sunlight.

"With six million, you could buy an awful lot," Adam told him. "Buy a dozen silly cars just like that one. You'd be the cock of the walk. And make the newspapers and everything. You'd get to wave that big fake check on the news. But I think you crossed the line with my friend here."

"What? What?" Mike squealed, playing dumb, his arms outstretched.

"The awful things you said on the phone all those times."

The brute came closer.

"Stay back."

He stopped. "Oh come on. Who the hell cares? Fifty grand'll fix anything."

"Nobody talks to her like that."

"Seriously, guy? I mean, goin' all noble on me now?"

"You heard me."

"And for her? Broad's only out for herself."

"Fuck you. I've heard enough. Nope, we're done talkin' here. We are done."

Mike Smith agreed. In fact, he was happy to take action. Realizing this, Adam passed the pants to Lori and told her to run. Mike Smith started after her. She built a lead, of course, but the laws of physics were on his side: her legs were short and his were not. And so in just six or seven seconds he was near enough to bring her down and jack those jeans and seize the ticket, and he'd have done all of that if not for a separate lunge performed by the nimbler Adam Durham, who clutched Mike Smith by the waist and held on tightly through all kinds of bucking and twisting, like someone's nephew trying to tackle a fullback. Soon Lori was fifty feet away and backtracking in smaller steps as she watched the battle. When she saw Mike Smith break free of Adam, she turned and took off again, head down, heels afire. Like a dog savoring the scent of human panic, the brawny man charged after her, growling, gasping, gaining speed, gaining ground, and it's a safe bet he never expected to be caught from behind a second time, but that's precisely what happened. Adam lunged and clutched an ankle, and this time both men went down hard on the pavement, where they scuffled and clawed, pushed and pulled, and gripped and gouged until the stronger man got the advantage. He sat upon Adam, crotch on crotch, his red-soaked face the picture of fury. He was smart enough to know the ticket was beyond his reach forever, and so all he could seek was a consolation prize, which would come in the form of rearranging this pretty boy's face. With his left paw he held the pretty boy's shoulder. With his right arm he hauled off.

From her safe distance, Lori Nelson screamed. It was a long, long scream, one begun in horror but ending in elation as she witnessed the first miracle of her life: a larger paw catching the offensive fist just in time. The paw belonged to a hulking stranger, a Boo Radley of Kansas, and this stranger used his other paw to drag Mike Smith to his feet, and then off his feet.

The stranger said, “You must be Smith.”

“He is!” shouted Adam, rising and backing away at the same time. “Thanks man, thanks! Nice to meet you!” He pushed out a thumbs-up and then raced off and met Lori halfway across the parking lot. Their adrenaline took them to the Camry with remarkable speed. They collapsed against it.

A breathless Adam spoke first. “Who was that masked man?”

“I don’t think it was a mask.”

She pushed the jeans into his arms. He popped a hand into the back pocket. He looked into her eyes as his trembling hand brought the wisp of paper into the sunlight. Lori offered a hand of her own to steady his.

“Well I’ll be,” he soon said, looking up from the ticket and into her eyes once again.

Lori wrapped an arm around his waist and cozied up against him. He kissed the top of her head.

“So, how do you feel now?” she murmured.

He lifted his lips from her lovely crown. “Good.”

“Me too. Real good.”

***

In their dark living room, Fabrizio Leone and Scotty O’Connor glared in the general direction of the TV set, which aired a pro football game. With each passing hour, the housemates grew more certain they’d sent Lenny Buck on a ridiculous goose chase and that the money they’d advanced him would be another total loss. They also feared he might kill somebody.

“Fobb, you know, sometimes I swear I think it’s fixed.” Scotty kicked down the footrest and leaned forward, his chin in his hands.

“What happened? A rip-off penalty? I wasn’t paying attention.”

“No. Not these games. Life, Fobb. I’m talkin’ about life. I mean, how come guys like us never end up winning? How come you and me are gonna have things suck for the rest of our lives and this cheatin’ Mike Smith gets to eat rib-eye steaks every night? I mean, damn, we never win.”

“Hey, no, when you put it like that, it makes us sound like losers. I refuse to become a loser.”

“I hear yuh, but it’s hard, man. I mean, it’s tough. I mean to say, it ain’t easy at all.”

“Don’t ever quit. You quit, then they win for sure and you might just end up hatin’ yourself some more. We keep on fightin’ and it keeps us busy and that’s good. So, like, enough with the gloom already. I can’t take any more gloom outta you. Why don’t you open up them curtains and you’ll see it’s still daytime out there. You’ll see the sun still shines in the sky.”

Scotty lifted, leaned, and reached for the curtains.

"Keep 'em shut, man! Damn, you know that bright shit kills my eyes."

Scotty shrugged and plopped back down. The plop made a terrific noise; it sounded like the recliner might break into four pieces and collapse outward, leaving the man suspended in midair. But a certain slapping sound a half-moment later is what got their attention.

"Someone at the door?"

Scotty leaned and peeped through the curtain. "I saw somethin' movin' out there." He rose and tramped around his chair and around the couch and made it to the storm door. He opened it and noticed a bulging envelope near his feet.

"Hey!" Scotty said. "Good news maybe!"

Fabrizio sprang from the couch and got to the package before Scotty could bend all the way down and get it. There in the brilliant, painful sunlight, the twerp stripped open the envelope with such ferocity that wisps of cash splashed all around him and fluttered down, down, down. Scotty dropped to a knee and tried to catch as much of the money as he could before it came back to earth.

***

The TV in Lori Nelson's living room flickered the early evening news, but the volume was muted, which was perfectly sensible because she and Adam Durham were much more interested in one another, cuddling on the carpeted floor, their shoulders against the base of her couch, their four hands eager to find a purpose.

Adam made use of his right hand by pointing at the TV. "Hey, I sort of know them!"

The news camera zoomed on a wizened geezer in an old-time hat, and then onto his shrunken, grimacing wife. They squinted joylessly through a thousand camera flashes as they held the big cardboard check like a burden.

"You know them?"

"They were in line just in front of me, the lucky bastards. He bought a pretty big wad of tickets. No wonder they won. How do you like that? I told you I was there when the winner was sold."

"They look sweet," she mused, taking his left hand and squeezing it between both of hers. "I so hope the money doesn't change 'em."

"I don't think it has time to."

"Wait, it's like an interview now. Turn it up. Where's that remote?"

When the audio kicked in, the old-timer was in mid-sentence. ". . . and if not for him, we'd still be half broke and eating tuna every day," the geezer said. "My hat is off to Mister Ian Moon. M-O-O-N."

"Ian Moon?" Lori said. "Our Ian Moon?"

“He gives a seminar on how to win the lottery. Apparently there are algorithms involved. Life is strange sometimes.” Adam muted the TV again and then reached and let the fingers of his right hand creep down her back, inch by inch, dangerously approaching ass-latitude.

She looked sidelong at him.

“What is it now?” he asked, innocently.

“I still think this whole thing was just an elaborate trick to get inside my pants.”

THE END

www.ingramcontent.com/pod-product-compliance
Lightning Source LLC
LaVergne TN
LVHW050318160826
845677LV00014B/3457